INQUISITIVE ANGEL

Borgo Press Books by S. FOWLER WRIGHT

INQUISITIVE ANGEL

A Novel of Fantasy

by

S. FOWLER WRIGHT

THE BORGO PRESS

An Imprint of Wildside Press LLC

MMX

Publisher's Note: the original manuscript for this novel is missing pages 1 and 210-212, as noted in the text.

CHAPTER ONE

SPIRIT

[missing page 1 of the manuscript]

...meal, which they did not disdain to share, and that they proved to be bearers of a very pleasant message for him.

Indeed, the angels of that period appear to have been without initiative, or any art or industry of their own, and to have been mainly employed in the humble office of a primitive postal service. And even the creation of a later millennium, feathered and winged though they were, had no higher occupations than those of a church choir, and the really difficult art of steering without a tail.

Elya, however—a young angel with whom we are particularly concerned—belonged to a later species. She had an adventurous spirit, such as is natural to the young. She was gifted with an intelligence far surpassing (in some ways, though not in all) that of the Human Race. Her sense of equity, in particular, was highly developed. She had studied it with a fascination which rewarded itself, and as diligently as a law student must study law.

She had also a physical quality which was peculiar to her creation, and the envy of angels of more primitive patterns. She was not limited to the appearance of Abraham's tramps, nor to that of the later creation of the finely designed shoulder muscles which could manage both arms and wings. She had a fluidity of form which she could control to her own will, through a process of atomic transition (for that which appears miraculous must always have a logical explanation) such as our own knowledge of atomic structure and flexibility can partially, but not thoroughly, comprehend.

Her sense of equity having led to a heavenly escapade which (apart from the indiscretions involved) would not be easily explicable in our limited language, the Archangel Gabriel, who had considerable authority over her junior creation (though they called him a black number when he was sufficiently far away) instructed her that it would be well to make herself scarce in Heaven for a short period, and her sense of equity giving this direction the force of a command, she decided to pay a visit to the Solar System where the varieties of sentient life on the planet Earth excited her curiosity, with the result that she appeared in Oxford Street, London, England, on the sunny afternoon of the Eighth of May 1953, having the discretion to assume the form of a small dog, after observing the unwillingness of *Homo sapiens* to exhibit themselves to each other *al fresco,* and the control of her own appearance not extending to provision of the apparel without which she would have been unlikely to perambulate peacefully in a London street.

In this humble but active guise she wandered for an hour of delirious wonder through the crowded traffic, until, seeing a variety of ladies' garments in the window of one of the thoroughfare's largest stores, she decided to enter it, and obtained such clothing as she might require, to enable her to stand erect on her hind legs, as men and angels are accustomed to do, without exciting the hostility of those around her.

She slipped in through a rotating door, but soon found that it was difficult to learn much while remaining unnoticed, and that her presence was of an extreme unpopularity.

After much chasing, during which she restrained with difficulty a canine impulse to bite the calves of her persecutors, she gained an undiscovered refuge behind a large window curtain, and considered without satisfaction the dilemma to which she had fallen.

She did not like being a dog. Her sight was poor, and she disliked having to judge everything round her by sense of smell, as it had become necessary to do. She was becoming acutely hungry, having necessarily assumed a dog's interior, as well as its outward aspect. She would have given much for a bone.

She got over this last difficulty with her usual mental agility by changing herself into another dog which had been more recently fed.

Having done this, she had leisure to develop plans, and to consider, in the first place, whether a dog was the best thing to continue to be.

It was evident that, with her present exterior, she could not examine the merchandise in the store with the freedom of movement which she desired. In the street no one had noticed her at all. So long as she were active to avoid wheels and legs, she could go where she would. But it was different here, and while she had intelligence enough to see reason for that, consolation did not result.

Then what should she do? If she could assume a form similar to that of one of the less unattractive of the bipeds who infested the store, she knew that she would be free to move as she would, as soon as she had clothed herself from the ample resources around her. But there was the awkward period of transition to be overcome. Could she hope to survive that?

She thought correctly that a young woman in a condition of nudity searching for attractive underclothing would excite even more lively attention than her canine presence had already done, though she was unsure what its exact nature might be. That attempt must wait for a quieter hour.

But meanwhile was a dog the best she could do?

She had already realised that it was impossible to become any creature without its attributes being hers. As a dog, she was conscious of impulses which her judgement did not approve. She remembered St. Paul (who was too fond of quoting passages from his own works) saying: "The things which we would not, those we do." It was an aphorism which applied *in excelsis* to an angel in a dog's body, and it was a state of affairs which should not be avoidably prolonged.

But what form should she prefer? She had admired a horse in the street, but its size would distend the curtain to an extent which might draw undesired attention; and would a horse's impulses be better than those she had?

Suppose she should become passionately desirous of carrying a man on her back? It was an idea of which she did not approve.

Suppose she should become something small? An insect? Or perhaps a spider? That would be better. More intelligent, she believed. But insects can be easily, even unintentionally, be crushed by larger creatures, and that raised an unpleasant doubt. What effect would it have on herself, if one of her (temporarily intended) incarnations should be destroyed? With a natural irritation, she had to admit to herself that she did not know.

Her mind turned to another doubt. If, when she were a dog, a dog's nature affected hers, as it certainly did, would the same law apply if, or rather, she should gain the form of a girl? Following this thought, she was led to wonder whether these incarnations were really new, or did she enter the body of an already existing dog? Particularly, should she become a girl, would she be entirely herself, or mingled with one already of carnal humanity?

Every intelligence must come in time to the frontiers of its own range, which it is unpleasant to do. Her knowledge was extensive, her intelligence keen. She knew (for instance) very much about the sentient inhabitants of the planet to which she had come. She could have differentiated accurately among a hundred thousand insect species. But this question of identity, as that of surviving destruction in an alien form, she must admit that she could not solve.

Perhaps, she thought hopefully, she could have resolved these enigmas if she had not been a dog. And might there not be warning in that? Suppose she should rashly incarnate herself in a creature of particularly low intelligence—might she not lose consciousness of that which she really was?

It was a most disconcerting doubt, however unlikely it may have been, and the question of becoming an insect, or even a spider, met a decided no.

She would retain her canine form until she could acquire that of humanity, with the covering which it so quaintly requires, and she would do this as promptly as could be contrived.

With this decision, she became aware that there was a momentary silence around her. She pushed out her head, and saw an empty aisle and a flight of stairs on its further side. Stairs are little used in the large stores where lifts are available. The dash she made was unobserved.

Standing for a moment at the top of the stairs, she saw an assistant serving a customer, neither of whom turned their eyes towards her. They were examining an evening frock. The department of feminine dress was here, which was something gained, for that which had been left had displayed toilet articles, ironmongery, and kitchen utensils, which would have been of little immediate use.

She crossed quickly to a dark and narrow space between two counters, into which she must introduce herself backward, as there would not have been space to turn, and settled down to wait till closing time should arrive, and she could acquire a more satisfactory shape.

Having further time for thought, distracted only by the fact that she was now troubled by fleas which she could not reach, her sense of equity was annoyed by another doubt. Would it be right to take garments for which she was so clearly unable to pay?

She pondered this vexatious point while the hours passed, and customers came and went, until she observed a woman advance silently down the aisle, glancing right and left, but rather as one who avoids observation than seeking service.

Being satisfied that she was alone, she made a swift movement toward a stand on which a rose-coloured dressing gown was displayed, and stuffed it into a large bag which hung emptily from her arm.

Elya, observing this, was unaware that she had given a low growl. But she saw the woman start violently at the sound, and then, as nothing further happened, her courage returned, and, with a quick nervous movement, she swept up a number of other garments, of less weight than value, such as are commonly described as undies or scanties by those that wear them, and was in the act of pushing them into the bag, when Elya, whose angelic and canine codes were alike outraged by what she saw, barked furiously, and made a sudden rush forward, at which the startled shoplifter threw down the damning evidence of the bag, and ran incontinently away.

The noise brought half a dozen people, assistants and customers, to the spot, but, before that, Elya had recovered her self-control and pushed rapidly backward into her former refuge.

She watched the picking up of the bag, and the examination of its contents. She saw the stores detective arrive on the scene, make a list of the purloined articles, order that they should be returned to their places, and go off with the bag.

She saw the assistants reverently smoothing out creases and refolding articles too delicate for the treatment they had received, and, as she did so, she saw the answer to the doubt she had had before.

Having done so signal a service, for which she could not put in a claim for remuneration in an orthodox manner, was she not equitably entitled to repay herself to an equal degree?

It was, at least, a debating point, and if it were subject to the qualification that she could scarcely clothe herself adequately without taking more than she had saved, was it not a possible reply that the shoplifter might have been deterred from other thefts on a later day?

Anyway, even a specialist in equity should not be *too* fussy, especially in one of those cases which come under the interstellar proverb that necessity knows no law.

CHAPTER TWO

RESULTS OF AN OVERSIGHT

It was about nine-thirty next morning when a young woman of singular charm and beauty, and dressed with the discrimination of those who have ample choice and heavenly judgement in what they do, approached the lift on the first floor, and was taken down by an attendant who looked at her curiously, and then, as she left, crooked a finger toward the store detective and pointed after her in a way which he instantly understood.

Elya was passing through a swing door into Oxford Street when she was addressed with a deferential suavity which would not have deceived anyone with the brains of a hen, even though fortified with a better conscience than a specialist in equity could be expected, under the circumstances, to have.

"Will madam kindly let me see the bill for the dress that she has just bought?"

"I haven't just bought one," she replied, with the simple truth which is often so much more confusing than many lies. "Why should you think that I have?"

"That," he replied, with a prosaic which was no comfort to her, "was what I wanted to know. I didn't think as you had."

Elya turned on him a smile which would have captivated any of the six directors of the firm (the seventh was a woman), but a store detective who could be vanquished by female wiles would not keep his job for a week. He said: "When we sell a frock here, we always take off the ticket."

"But you didn't sell it. I've just told you that," she answered, with the patient sweetness of one who endures folly without offence, at which he gave up the verbal duel, and said curtly: "Perhaps you'll come into the office. I suppose you don't want to be given into custody in the street?"

"I don't mind going into your office with you, if you think that will do any good," she replied, with the exasperated consciousness that she was not handling the position to a satisfactory end. But she was restricted in her technique by the knowledge that the price ticket was not only on the dress she wore, but on most, if not all, of the undergarments which she had requisitioned for the assertion of her respectability. In short, she was aware that she had been a simple absolute fool, which even angels dislike to know.

She was led into a private office, where an austere female of mature years gazed at her with glassy eyes.

"Another, Barton?" she said.

"Yes, madam. Ticket still on the back," he said grimly.

"It will save time," she said to Elya, in a tone of ice, "if you take it off. I suppose you've got your own underneath."

"I'm not wearing two dresses, if you mean that."

"Then you'd better tell Barton where you've hidden your own, and he'll fetch it, unless you prefer to go to jail in your underwear."

"I told him—," Elya began, and then stopped with the consciousness that the game was lost unless it should be played in a different way. Those price tickets beneath her skirts!

The astonished manageress saw the clothes collapse into a heap on the floor.

She gazed at them with a white face, and a slack jaw. "Where the…? What the…?" she began; and then "Barton, did she slip through the door?"

But madam, conscious as she stooped that she was being bitten by a most vicious flea, could find nothing under the desk.

"Barton," she said. "I'm not blaming you, but she's tricked us somehow. You'd better phone for the police."

As she spoke, she struck at her cheek, from which something leapt. She said: "Barton, there must have been a flea in those clothes. Look, there it is."

She struck out wildly, lost sight of the leaping pest, and forgot what she had been doing at the astounding sight of a nude young woman seated in relaxed comfort in her own chair.

"You shameless hussy! she gasped. "You'll get six months for this. Barton—" But it was no use calling on Barton now, for the detective had left the room.

Elya gazed at the outraged woman with a recovered placidity. "It's not my fault," she said. "You would have it this way. I wasn't going to be slapped down by you. But as for being ashamed of how you were made, don't you think it's rather blasphemous? I don't wonder you call it the fall of man. And yet, of course..."—for her sense of equity supervened—"...if I had your figure I shouldn't feel just as I do."

She spoke dispassionately, for though many human oddities may be duplicated in celestial regions, the wearing of clothes has never had popular support, and even votaries of paint would be hard to find. (The nightgowns worn by the singing angels when performing to earthly audiences are a gesture of politeness only.)

"Of course," she added equably, "I'll put them on again if you like. But I'd better take off the tickets."

The bewildered woman, horribly conscious that one of the directors might enter the room at any minute, and that she would have great difficulty in giving any satisfactory and plausible explanation of what had occurred, made no objection to this.

Elya dressed in a composed manner, removing the price tickets as she did so, and putting them in a neat heap on the lady's desk.

She left without further opposition, giving a friendly word in passing to the astonished Barton, but she had the sense to see that she could not continue such escapades without catastrophe. "I must play this game," she thought, "from now on in a different way."

CHAPTER THREE

MAINLY CONVERSATION—AND CAKES

Elya walked toward Bond Street, pondering what she should do next, but in the most contented mood that she had yet known.

She was not entirely satisfied with her own behaviour, which had not been conspicuous either for dignity or logic, and she did not intend that her youthful levity should give Gabriel just occasion for any of his sneering, old-fashioned remarks when they should meet again, as she knew they must.

But, by whatever means, she had obtained the clothes to which the human biped so closely clings—and very good ones they were!

Also, now that she had the use of a human brain, instead of that of a dog, she saw some things clearly which had been hazy before. She did not inhabit the body of any pre-existent young woman. She was in every way self-made, and herself alone. Even a dog should have been able to deduce that, from the process of atomic change through which her metamorphoses were contrived. She would never be one again. But there had been real fun in being a flea! Only the sudden terror she had felt when the beastly woman began slapping about would have availed to put so abrupt an end to that joyous bout.

Now she must adjust her mind to the higher grades of existence on this queer planet she had come so far to explore. And first she must get a meal.

Fortunately, the difficulty of money did not arise, for, when she had chosen her clothes, she had also presented herself with a *de luxe* handbag, which contained a purse and a pound note. Certainly, she had not paid herself for her services in scaring the shoplifter in a too-niggardly spirit.

Now she went in to Bustard's, took a seat near the windows of the first-floor room, so that she could overlook the traffic while she ate, and ordered coffee and cakes, after she had been disappointed by the information that lunch was not yet being served.

She had not sat there long, enjoying and marvelling at the sights below her, before a young man, dark-haired, brown-eyed, and lean of build, sat down at her table.

His self-excuses for this intrusion were that the room was rather full and that a window seat is attractive when the sun shines, as it did on May 9, 1953, that being the day with which we are now concerned. His reason was that she was in fact, as well as by his own assessment, the loveliest girl he had ever seen.

He ordered coffee, watched her take her third pastry from a plate which had held eight, and took one himself.

She looked at him very much as the store detective had looked at her, decided that men existed for other purposes than a needless quarrel, took a meringue of particularly repulsive appearance, and said indifferently: "Oh, well, we can order more."

Uncertain of whether he had been rebuked for an unintentional liberty, but glad of any conversational opening, he answered randomly: "Oh, yes, they're good cakes you get here. But I suppose they're not very digestible. Not more than one—or...," he added hastily, with a belated consciousness that the remark might be taken in a too-personal way, "or perhaps two."

She looked at him coldly. "My digestion is perfect," she said simply as though mentioning a fact which should have been evident without words.

"Yes," he answered, "I'm sure everything is," and was again aware that it might not be developing the conversation in the best way.

She answered without taking offence, but in the same tone of one who deals with matters too obvious to be discussed: "There's nothing wrong with my lungs, if you mean that."

For a practising barrister, even in the first year, he was not showing the adroitness that the occasion required. But while he paused, in momentary doubt of how best such a conversation could be continued, she showed that she had no intention of letting it drop, by looking down into the street, and saying: "I've been marvelling at how many cars there are. Why does everyone move about?"

He looked surprised. He said: "London's always like that. I suppose you have just come into town. But I should say that most cities are much the same."

"Well, it's new to me," she replied. "I've just come from—abroad."

Wondering where the home of such loveliness might be found, and combining flattery with a quest for this information, he said: "Your country must be worth visiting, if the first introduction be any guide. But that would be too much to hope."

"Meaning you like my looks? But I was different then. Only an impudent youngster who made Gabriel lose his hair."

Wondering still more at this intimate and yet baffling glimpse into her family life, and whether Gabriel were elder brother or husband (but there was no ring on her hand!), he went on: "Are you going to bless us by living here now, or is it only a short visit?"

"Oh, I wouldn't say that! I expect to stay quite a while. I've come too far to go back without seeing anything. And besides—"

She tantalised him with the unfinished sentence, breaking off to call a passing waitress to bring another plate of pastries and cakes. Then she turned the conversation again to the traffic that moved below.

"I think they drive very skilfully. I expect there'd be an accident but for that."

"Well, there are a good many."

"Many *accidents*? Not serious ones? Surely they'd stop it at once, if there were?"

"People don't look at it in that way. It is regarded as essential to modern life."

"They can't really believe that. You mean wherever anyone is, he wants to be somewhere else? Then why not get there and make the cars into cupboards or something else really useful? And if they do all want to get somewhere else, they're not really having a good try. Do you notice that most of the cars are half empty, although there are crowds walking the same way?"

"Well, the cars are not theirs."

"Still, I should have thought they'd have found some way to stop them and get in. I'm sure I shall love your country. I didn't know that the whole universe had anything quite so quaint."

"It could be argued, no doubt, though it is a somewhat unusual view. I suppose you come from one where the customs are very different?"

"I should say I do! Why, we used to make hoops which—but I should never make you understand about that."

"You could try."

"I don't think I could. But you're eating nothing." She glanced at him with sudden sympathetic concern: "Oh, but you told me. You've got something wrong with your inside."

Resenting a charge for which there was really very little foundation, he said: "Oh, no. I didn't mean that," and took a macaroon sandwich which cleared the dish, while she asked: "Have you got a car?"

"No, I'm sorry I haven't."

"That's a pity. I thought you could have taken me here and there."

"I should have been delighted. I may say I shall be. My father has two, and I can always borrow one for a week. He lives near Godalming. I should have to go down and fetch it."

"I don't know where Godalming is, but it sounds as though you live somewhere nearer than that. Have you got a house?"

"I've got a flat on the Embankment. I hardly need a house, being alone."

"Well, I suppose there'll be room for two."

He controlled surprise. He said: "You mean you'd like me to put you up?"

"Yes, of course. You see I've only got a pound, and that was just for luck; and it gets colder at night, I've found that out already. I know people don't give others the things they've got without having money for them. Gabriel made me learn that, and a lot more. He said he didn't want me to disgrace him, as well as myself."

"You mean you're without money, and quite alone?"

"Well, I couldn't have brought it with me, could I? And no one else wanted to come."

Leonard Weyleigh became silent. He knew that if he were required to give counsel's opinion upon the position, or to obtain it from a more experienced barrister, it would be that prudence required retreat.

Did she intend to return with him to his flat, practice alluring ways, and rob him while he slept of all the money and portable valuables that were his?

Her bold approach was suggestive of this, in more ways than one. And yet was "bold" quite the right word? Was it not rather casual or matter-of-fact? Nor could he say that she practised seductive ways. From first to last, her eyes had been on the cakes rather than him. He could not say the same of his own, which had been mainly on her. And it was an occupation he liked. But for Laura—

and convention, of course. But what on earth was he to do or say?

As the conversation paused thus, and her eyes wandered to the street again, as though having lost interest in a decided thing, he became aware that the waitress was hanging round, with a small tablecloth in her hand. He saw that the room was now almost empty, and that most of the tables had been laid for lunch. She said: "If you've quite finished, perhaps—?"

Elya turned her eyes from the street. She said: "Oh, yes, we've finished. You can take them," pointing to the empty cake dishes. She picked up her bag, rising to go, and then stayed. "Oh, but you're laying lunch, aren't you? Then it might be silly to go."

The girl, who was making out separate bills for two who had not come in together, said: "Yes, madam," with indifferent politeness, and then: "How many cakes, sir?" And learning that Leonard had only eaten two, she looked at the plates in calculating astonishment. But facts are facts, and it was certainly no part of her duty to criticise the appetites of the customers.

Elya looked at her bill as the waitress removed the crockery. She was of a practical mind, and would not welcome a second encounter with the legal customs of her new world. She said: "I didn't know it would be this much. Shall I have enough left for lunch?"

Leonard Weyleigh, who had risen uncertainly, it being much earlier than he was accustomed to take a midday meal, but being conscious of a strong disinclination to go, though fully aware of the awkwardness of the position into which she was steering him, said: "I suppose it would depend upon how much lunch you have."

She became aware that he had risen, and dealt with the more immediate issue. "Oh, but you're not going? If you do, I shall have to come."

Did he wish that? Not, at least, without some plan, some appreciation of where it might lead. He sat down, saying: "Well, it's rather early for lunch, but, if that's an invitation, I won't decline."

"It's not exactly an invitation, because you may have to pay for both, but of course I didn't want you to go."

"I think I could manage that."

"Then there's no reason you shouldn't stay. You can tell me what's best for our insides, and about your flat, and what I'll need to get for tonight. Oh, and that'll mean money again. What a nuisance to everyone all this paying must be. I wonder they haven't decided to give it up long before now."

"It would not be a simple matter," he answered. "But surely money is not unknown in your own country?"

He thought he had found an opening here which would lead to the information that he desired; and so it may be said that it did, for when she exclaimed with wonder: "Of course, we don't have money. What use would it be to us?" and he answered with the straight question: "Could you tell me where the country is where money is not required?" she replied: "Yes, it's about three million miles beyond Sirius, and the second turn to the left."

But he found no satisfaction in that. He said: "Well, of course, if you don't want to tell me! But I suppose it was bad manners to ask."

"It wasn't bad manners at all. But what's the use of saying things that you won't believe?"

"I could try."

"Then will it be any use if I say it again?"

"I didn't mean jokes like that."

"Suppose we talk about it some other time."

"That's for you to say. The first question is what you're going to do after lunch. Haven't you really any means of getting money at all? I mean traveller's cheques, or anything like that."

"No. How could I? I know what you mean. You'd probably be surprised at how many things I *do* know. But there are lots that I don't. I've seen that already. More than I should have thought there could possibly be. You see the difficulty was that I wasn't sure where—I mean what part of the world—I should come to, and I had to learn lots and lots of things that may be no use at all."

Failing to make sense of this, and being roused by a feeling that she must think he could be bamboozled by tricky words, which any barrister would resent, though they should come (as they did) from the loveliest lips in the land, he resolved to challenge her with all the skill that he had.

He said: "You must at least have decided on coming to this country, or you would not have acquired our language to such perfection—unless you come from one of the Dominions, or the United States, where travellers' cheques would be very easy to get."

"I don't know whether you're really serious when you say that," she answered, looking at him with smiling eyes, which lightened the discourtesy of her words, "but it doesn't sound sense to me.

"I learnt English because it's talked over half the Earth—I'm not wrong about that, am I?—and I learnt Chinese also, and Russian and Spanish and French; and it seemed likely that one of those would be all I should need to know. You couldn't expect me to learn all the hundreds of languages which are talked by small nations, which I shouldn't be likely to need."

"Well," he said, with little purpose beyond keeping up the conversation, for the more she talked the more certain she would be to slip, "if you learnt to speak them all as well as you do English, I shouldn't think you've done much else from the day you were born."

"But I wasn't—," she began, and checked herself with the realisation that she had already gone too far with incredible assertion. "The real question is what I'm going to do about money now."

"Do you mean you know Russian as well as you do English?"

"Yes. Why not? I just know it."

"And how to speak it?"

"Yes, of course."

"And Chinese."

"Yes."

"Can you *write* Chinese?"

"Yes. You have to know how to write languages. I saw that."

Leonard had had a wild idea. He almost spoke it. But was it likely she would? And besides, it was an incredible tale. What he had to do was to *convict* her of some falsehood which would drive her into frank confession, or give him courage to walk out on her, as he knew that he ought to do. He saw that he must try again. He said: "Well here's the menu."

He found that she read its queer mixture of English and pseudo-French without difficulty, though she referred to him as to which dishes he would advise her to choose. He thought: "She hasn't come from any remote land where these languages were unknown. More likely Shaftesbury Avenue, or Soho." But was there much explanation in that?

CHAPTER FOUR

AN INVITATION TO LINCOLN'S INN

Delicately, with a sure accuracy of touch at which he must wonder, Elya was peeling a ripe pear.

The rind, transparently thin, fell from the knife in a long spiral which did not break, and curled on the plate beneath.

While lunch had progressed, and she had been largely occupied in its consumption, he had had leisure to think, and had formed a plan which gratified foolish desire, and which he yet felt to be cautious and sound.

His friend Bentley, who rented the flat immediately above his own, had just gone on a three weeks' holiday, leaving him the key, so that he could forward letters, or deal with any business which might arise.

There was a notice on the door that Mr. Bentley, who rented the flat, was away until the 27th, and that callers should apply at No. 9 below. If Miss __ (he could surely ask for her name, which should be some indication of nationality) should be put up there for one night (he would undertake nothing more), it was most unlikely that she would be disturbed, and improbable that her presence would be observed.

He felt it to be a good plan. Cautious. Prudent. Even the conventions would be observed. And it gave further time for probing the mystery of this amazing girl, so familiar yet so remote, which he was determined to do.

He put the plan to her, and found that it was well, though somewhat casually, received.

He said: "Then if that's how it's to be, we'd better know each other's name. Mine's Leonard Weyleigh."

"Mine's Elya."

"And after that?"

"There's no need to change it, is there?"

"I didn't mean that." (He was aware of some ambiguity in the way he had put it. He certainly hadn't meant that she should change it for his.) "I meant: what is your second name."

"Do I need two here?"

"It's usual to have a surname. If you understand the language, you must know that."

"Yes. I suppose I did. I knew people have more than one. But I hadn't thought of it. Is it a law? Not for visitors, I suppose."

"Not exactly. But you can surely make use of your father's name?"

"Oh, you mean I could be Fitz-something. Yes, I see. But I never had—" (But it wouldn't do to say that.) "Would Fitz-Gabriel do?"

"I don't see why it shouldn't, if it's the truth."

For obvious reasons, she made no answer to that. He thought at first that he had learnt little, or nothing. But did not the name of Gabriel tell him a good deal? It implied possible Teutonic, but more probable Latin descent. Say European, going perhaps a long way back, her ancestors having wandered to other lands. But he still told himself that it was the Charing Cross Road, more likely than not.

He called for the bill, examined the contents of his wallet, and handed her two pounds, saying: "You'll need these, if you've really got no luggage. I expect you'll need more, but it's honestly all I can spare."

She answered: "You're being really kind to me. I'm glad I met you. But I'm sure I shall be able to pay you back, when I've had time to look round."

For the first time, she looked at him in a direct personal way. He saw gratitude in her eyes, but recognised (was he pleased?) that she was still of an aloof unemotional mood. Pulchritude there certainly was, but of its practical uses, no trace at all.

"I've got to get back now," he said. "I've got some pleadings to settle before midday tomorrow, and there are one or two points about which I'm more shaky as to what the law is than I should like my clients to guess. But it may be best in every way for you to come back with me first, and get settled in."

She answered, with a quick grasp of the implication of what he said, which confirmed his opinion that she had been born within two miles of the vortex of human misery on the north side of Fleet Street: "Oh, you mean you're a fighting lawyer. It must be fun for you, though I suppose it's rather different for those who get fleeced. Of course, we'll go back at once, and you must forget I exist. I expect I've hindered you too much as it is."

She spoke with such transparent sincerity that he gained confidence in her indifference to himself. Without feeling entirely pleased, he said: "Perhaps it's a case for a taxi." If she should behave discreetly in that sheltered propinquity, this judgement would be confirmed, though with no diminution of the enigma of what she was. And, as to that, he soon had to recognise that even a jury of Victorian matrons would have agreed that propriety had been fully observed.

Arriving at their destination, he led her up a narrow spiral stone stairway to a small landing which had three numbered doors, one of which bore his name in white letters: Mr. Leonard Weyleigh.

He had taken the key from his pocket, but put it back, with a frown of puzzled annoyance, when he saw that his door was slightly open. He knew who must be inside, and foresaw an interview of inevitable difficulty, but it was too late to draw back.

CHAPTER FIVE

"NO EARTHLY EXPLANATION"

As Leonard stepped aside to enable Elya to go first into the room, she met the lady who was already there; without precedent introduction, and ignoring (if she were aware of) that conventional necessity, she spoke at once, with the freedom that heavenly nature inclined her to use.

"Hullo! Leonard said that there'd be no one here. But I think that I shall get on all right with you. At least, I'm not quite sure that I shall."

Laura Bentley—a blue-eyed blonde, who knew herself to be as attractive by earthly standards as most men would desire—gave no answer to this surprising frankness; and Leonard, who had now entered the room, said hurriedly: "Of course, I couldn't guess you'd be here. This is Miss Laura Bentley. Laura, this is Elya. She's just come from abroad. I'm sure you'll get on splendidly."

Laura felt constrained to hold out her hand. She said, in a tone which would have held no conviction to female ears: "Yes, of course. Glad to meet you. Did you have a good journey? Len, you never told me you'd got a sister."

"Elya isn't my sister. I only met her two hours ago. I've got to put her up somewhere. She's only just got into town, and has nowhere to go."

During the thirty seconds of silence that followed, he was conscious that the explanation had a queer sound. But what *could* he say that Laura would not be certain to misunderstand—or perhaps understand too well? And meanwhile the two had looked at each other, and learnt more than men might have done in as many years, and if Laura still had a bewildered mind, there were exceptional excuses for that.

Laura, who made judicious and moderate use of the cosmetics which have been developed from ancestral woad, and are in such common use that few, either women or men, would have regarded her as being painted at all, thought: "It *can't* be natural. But what *on earth* does she use?"

That anything on earth didn't limit the enquiry was unlikely to suggest itself in explanation. Complimenting the Western Hemisphere beyond its extreme worth, her thoughts went to New York. Without enthusiasm, she recognised that she was looking at the loveliest girl she had ever seen. And she was somehow so *new*. And so were here clothes. As though they had all been put on for the first time. Who *on earth* could she be? And what brought her here?

And meanwhile Elya was fighting for self-control. She thought that she had no use for Laura, and it was transparently evident that Laura had none for her. She wasn't worried about that. Her trouble was an almost uncontrollable impulse to be a flea. And she knew that she had yielded perilously to that erratic inclination only a few hours earlier, and had then resolved not again to incur the hazard of being anything so small. And the woman's pursuing slaps! No, she must choose a better method than that.

And then she reminded herself that Leonard had said that he had work to do, and an impulse of generosity (for however impish she could be, she was of a fundamental kindliness) caused her to subdue her feelings to make use of the woman for his relief.

"Leonard," she asked, "hadn't Laura better come out with me to spend the two pounds, while you go on looking up law?"

Laura, almost grasping the effrontery of this suggestion, turned to Leonard to say: "I only called because Charles wrote to say that there might be a letter coming here from the Pensons, and he thought I'd better deal with it, instead of you sending it on to him. But there's nothing upstairs, and Wilson let me in, so that I could wait for you here. But I can see that you've got an…important case; and if there's no letter I'd better be getting on."

But Elya was not easy to put aside. Before Leonard could reply, she said: "I'm not his law case, if you mean that. But he's got work to do, and doesn't want to be hindered by us. He's putting me up for the night, and I want to buy some whatever—well, you'll know what I shall need. I don't see why it should take us more than an hour. But if he doesn't want me back so soon, you might have tea with me after that. I've got nearly three pounds, so it ought to do."

Laura, who was normally a good-natured girl, glared at her from eyes in which bewilderment fought with rage. Had she—had they all—gone *mad*?

Leonard was putting the intruder "up for the night"—whatever might be the meaning of that?—but wasn't it evident? And yet, *Leonard*! Of course, they hadn't expected to find her here, but as they had, they were making the most use of her that they could—she was to go out to buy a nightgown for the event!

"Unless," she said savagely, "you're *non compos mentis*, you're about the most brazen beast that I ever met."

Elya looked puzzled. She said: "I know I'm not a brazen beast, so I suppose I must be whatever else you're trying to say, but I don't know what it is."

She felt that something was wrong somewhere. With celestial thoroughness she had learnt the language, including about 50,000 technical words that she was unlikely to need, and half as many colloquialisms that she was more likely to hear, as they had been in use for a century past, but *non compos mentis* had no meaning for her. Had some jester played her a trick? She thought not, though she knew that such things did occur in her heavenly home. She would have developed the subject, but Laura was in no mood for discursive talk. She said curtly: "It means you're loony. I suppose you can understand that. And perhaps you'll be good enough to get out of the way."

She tried to push past Elya as she said that, making for the door, which, as they stood in that narrow room, was not easy to reach, unless Elya should move, or be pushed aside.

But she showed no inclination to give ground to this angry request. She appeared to justify the suggested description when she enquired, with more show of temper than had been aroused by any previous incident of earthly experience: "Should you dislike being bitten by a large flea? And where should you hate it most?"

How Laura would have replied to this enquiry is beyond knowledge, for Leonard interposed before the question had been completed. He caught Laura's arm as he exclaimed: "Look here, Laura, you're not going like that. You've got it all wrong. I'm simply lending Elya Charles' room for a night, because she's alone in London, and got nowhere to go. You can't say there's anything wrong in that. I'm sure if he were here—"

"Yes," Laura agreed, with no increase of friendliness in her voice, "I dare say he would! But would you mind giving me the lady's name. I'm not sufficiently familiar to address her as you are doing."

"Laura, don't be a pig! Can't you understand that Elya's a stranger to us? We don't want her to go back home with a report that no Londoner knows how to behave."

It would be too much—far too much—to imply that Laura responded to this appeal in a spirit which Leonard would have approved, but it seemed to have a curiously quietening effect. She became still for a moment, and then said, in a better modulated voice than before: "No, I won't be a pig. I'd rather learn what good manners are. You must just tell me what I'm to do. I'm to go out with Elya now and do some shopping. She wants everything a girl needs for the night, and we're to buy it all with two pounds, or perhaps three. Don't you think," she asked, as one anxious to solve a difficult problem in a practical way, "we'd better take a bus to the Whitechapel Road? I could manage the fares myself, and perhaps contribute a few shillings besides."

Leonard knew her too well to be deceived by this treacherous calm. He knew, at the very best, that it must mean later trouble for him. But, for the moment, it seemed to open a way of precarious peace. And he had already realised that the two pounds which he had tendered to relieve his inexplicable guest's financial stringency were inadequate. The trouble had been that there was not much more that his wallet held. And why should he give all he had to a stranger who had fastened herself upon him?

But it was difficult to harden his heart against that radiant indifferent loveliness, and certainly he could not allow them to take a bus to the East End. He supposed vaguely that the ladies who inhabit that part of London require transparencies for the night, and paint their faces when morning comes, but there was incongruity in the thought of Elya being supplied from the depots at which they shopped. He said: "You can't do that. Perhaps I'd better give you a cheque."

"It wouldn't be any good," Laura replied. "You know how far your bank is from here, and it's half past two now—and besides, I've got something else to do before midnight. But it doesn't matter," she added sweetly, "I've got an account at Dickens & Jones. I'll put everything down there."

CHAPTER SIX

LAURA HAS A BAD TIME

Laura had the natural jealousy of a girl who discovers her fiancé introducing another of surpassing loveliness to his flat, whom he tells her he only met two hours before, whom he only knows by her first name, and whom he has already arranged to "put up" for the night; and this natural jealousy was complicated by an equally natural resentment when the unknown spoke of and to her as of someone whom she could order about.

But she was fundamentally sensible, and this quality, supported by the intuition in which women are said to excel, warned her that there was something beyond the obvious—something *queer*—in the event upon which she had been an unexpected and unwelcome intruder. And even to think of herself as unwelcome required qualification. Her appearance had been embarrassing to Leonard. That had been easy to see, and equally so to explain, but she had not observed that it had roused in Elya any emotion at all.

"I'm to be used," she thought angrily, "if I can be helpful to her; but otherwise I might be a doormat to take the dirt off her shoes."

Divided thus between anger and bewilderment, and having observed that Elya was not reluctant to talk, she decided wisely that it would be best to encourage her to do so. "For though," she thought, "what she says may be mostly lies, more likely than not, I'll pretend to take it all in, and if I do that she'll give herself away in the end. Liars always do."

And while she came to this prudent resolve, she had the satisfaction of thinking that, whatever might be the truth of a puzzling affair, she had insured herself against being made the fool of the piece by her sweet-voiced decision that the purchases should be charged to her account. "If he's up to any monkey business," she thought, "that'll be something he'll find it hard to digest."

She led the way out, with Elya following on the narrow stair, and said, as they stood on the pavement together: "I wasn't kidding. I really am rather short of time. I think a taxi—"

"Oh, yes," Elya agreed readily. "I know all about them. I really know a good deal. They're where men expect you to kiss them. Leonard brought me in one. I think he was surprised that I didn't try."

With this light-hearted display of esoteric knowledge, she waved a white hand at a passing vehicle, and continued to develop the theme when they were seated within it.

"Of course, before I came, I'd learnt what men are like in all parts of the world. I expected him to take a quicker interest than he did, but I think he was rather scared. I don't suppose he'd met anyone quite so perfect before. I mean, look at your nose, and your left ear! Though," she added, with her natural courtesy, "I expect most women are worse than you. But what I hadn't expected was that I should have any feelings myself. It ought to be fun when I get back."

"Perhaps I ought to tell you that he is practically engaged to me."

"It's kind of you to warn me, of course. But I know that it doesn't always make much difference. I've learnt all about that too. And besides, *practically*! But you shouldn't look on it as quite a normal event. I may go back any time. And then he'll come to you to cheer him up, more likely than not."

"Do you mind telling me where you may be going back to?"

"Oh, I—I suppose I shouldn't have said what I did! I shouldn't mind telling you, but what use is it when I know I shan't be believed?"

"You can't tell that till you try."

"I tried with Leonard."

"Well, you seem to have him under control."

"Not because he believed what I said."

"And yet it was really true?"

"Yes, of course."

"Then perhaps I might, if you tell me that seriously."

"I don't think you could. It's the way your minds are made. You can't believe anything unless it's like something you've heard before."

"Who do you mean by that? Leonard and I?"

"I mean men and women. Not especially you."

"Including yourself, of course?"

"No. I'm different. That's what he couldn't—and I know you couldn't—believe."

"You can try me."

"Then I'll make it as simple as possible. I'll just say I'm not human. I've come from outside the Earth."

That was not what Laura had expected to hear. She had thought that she was dealing with an adventuress, who would try to fool her with clever lies. But she now revised that opinion. She was in contact with one to whom the description *non compos mentis* would not be one of vulgar abuse, but sober accuracy. A case for pity. And had Leonard known or guessed this? Perhaps a client whom he was trying to save from the mental home where she certainly ought to be? And would he have told her this had he had a private opportunity?

She saw that she might have done injustice in two directions at once; but the technique on which she had resolved might still be that which the occasion required.

She said: "Well, you're the one to know best about that. I don't see any reason why you should tell me what isn't true. How long have you been here?"

"Only since yesterday. I began by being a dog."

"And then you thought you'd like being a girl better?"

"Yes. I never meant to be anything else. But there was the trouble about the clothes. I was a flea for a few minutes, but I didn't mean to stay being that."

"It must have been rather fun."

"Yes, it was. I'd show you now, but there'd be the clothes left lying about; and there mightn't be time to put them on again before we should have to get out."

"I don't think I should try that now, if I were you. We're almost there, and the next question is whether you know what you want, or are you leaving it all to me?"

"I'll leave it to you, unless I see anything that I'd like to have. I don't want to have to do a lot of hunting about. I got these clothes without help, but you see I was alone in the store, and could sort everything, and think it over before I chose. You wouldn't say I did badly? Or perhaps I'm wrong about that?"

"I think you're beautifully dressed. But I wish you'd tell me what really did happen—I mean about being alone in the store."

"Well, I just was. I stayed there during last night. It was all quite simple except not taking the price tickets off. I don't like telling you that, because I was such a fool. But I never have told a lie. I expect I could, if I tried. I mean really well. You and Leonard tell lies all the time. I shouldn't like doing that. You keep on thinking what's best to say. But I got out of it rather well. It was then that I was the flea. I bit the woman about the face, and the detective thought he was seeing ghosts. Is this where we get out?"

The shopping gave Laura one of the worst times that her life had known.

Elya was very careful at first. She grudged spending eighteen pence. Wasn't there something cheaper than that? That was before she had realised what was meant by everything being put down to Laura's account. But when she did, she showed a disposition to buy everything of the best—that the shop held.

She told Laura that she had no reason to worry. She would pay for it all herself.

"I thought you hadn't got anything except the two pounds."

"I haven't now, but I shall."

"You mean some's being sent on?"

"No. Where should it be from? I mean I shall have it, like everyone else."

"Yes, but how?"

"I don't know. But I shall get some. Don't you see that everyone's got some. Do you think I shall be more stupid than anyone else?"

"But it's usual to get it first, and then spend it."

"You didn't say that when you explained about having an account. Anyway, I've not got it now, and I want the things."

Laura reflected with trepidation that her account had never been above seven pounds (or had it been eight last April?). She observed one department after another referring to the accounts office before passing the invoices. When Elya selected a dressing gown at thirteen guineas, she was not surprised when she was asked to have a word with the cashier.

"Madam," a firm-lipped, suave-tongued lady said pleasantly, "I thought you might like to know that your purchases are already over fifty pounds."

"Oh," she answered easily, "that's all right…"—and had a disconcerting memory as she spoke that Elya had said that she told lies all the time—"…that's all right. I'm not buying for myself. It's for a lady who's visiting London, and I've been asked to look after her."

"And she will be paying for them before she leaves?"

"No, I'm sure she won't. I shouldn't think of asking her. Mr. Leonard Weyleigh—I expect you know him; he's a barrister in the city—told me it would be all right if I had anything she wanted put down to my account. You needn't think you won't get your money, if you mean that."

"I haven't suggested anything of the kind. I see that your accounts have always been promptly settled. But I thought you ought to know how much you were running up. Do you mean that this Mr. Weyleigh will settle the bill?"

"You can ring him up if you like. But if he didn't, and it's only about fifty pounds, I've got enough in my own bank, so you needn't worry. But I'll tell her not to buy anything more."

"I didn't ask you to do that," the cashier replied, but there was still a doubt in her voice, and Laura thought it best to reply shortly: "Well, I shall anyway."

Actually, she felt relief that she had an excuse for stopping the buying bout. She remembered that the money in her bank was being slowly accumulated toward the requirements of what she had supposed to be an approaching marriage. So she hoped it might still be, but even if all were still well between herself and Leonard, it wouldn't be advanced by the money being spent for this stranger's clothes, and if Leonard had to pay it, it would be a distinction with no difference at all.

She was glad to go back to her angelic companion and tell her that further credit could not be taken, which Elya heard with her usual good humour, only looking to see how two pounds in cash could be spent before leaving the shop.

When they were in the street again, and had called a taxi, and a large number of cardboard boxes had been brought down and packed into it, she watched Elya settle herself in such space as remained, but did not join her. She gave Leonard's address to the driver, and said pleasantly to Elya: "No, I'm not coming back with you. Why should I? And, besides, I've got another appointment. I've done all that I was asked. I expect we shall be meeting again."

"Elya said: "Yes, I'm sure we shall," which was hardly what she would have preferred to hear, but it seemed likely.

CHAPTER SEVEN

FLIRTATION ON A NEW PLANE

The taxi disappeared in the traffic of Regent Street, and Laura went to a call-box. She rang up Leonard. She spoke without asperity, but as one who was entitled to an explanation which she intended to get. She said: "Well, I've just put Elya, or whatever you call her, into a taxi, and sent her back to you, as it seems to be where she belongs, or at any rate that's her idea of how the land lies. I've bought her about sixty pounds worth of flimsies, and dressing gowns, and other things. She's bringing them all along, so you'll be able to go over them with her in the next hour. By the way, you'll need someone to help carry the boxes upstairs, unless you're going to leave it to her. And you may like to know that she says that she stole everything she's got on during the last night at Bent & Westley's. She also said she'd turned into a flea because the price tickets were still on, so you may believe as much as you like. But if she came to you as a client, I should say you'll have a busy time, and a very useful lot of publicity thrown in. She didn't? Then I should like to know how she did. But anyway I should think that you'll soon be making enough money to marry someone, though I'm not sure who it's going to be. I don't think Elya would object to bigamy in the least, but I might. And, by the way, she wouldn't buy any cosmetics. She didn't seem interested. She's genuine so far. I'll give her that. But what else she is, heaven may know, but I don't. But for that, the bill might have been a hundred pounds, instead of sixty, and if I heard you say, "Oh, the devil!" when I told you this first, I should like to know what you expected to hear. Oh, and did I tell you she spent the two pounds, so you'd better slip out, and pawn something, or you'll have nothing for cigarettes, though I shouldn't say that she smokes, but if you're taking her out for dinner, I should say that you're in for a good bill. I *can* find all the sixty, but what I thought was that we might go half and half. You see—"

She was silenced at last by the exasperation of her fiancé's voice. "Laura, will you let me give you a few facts before you say any more things that you don't mean. I don't know the woman from Adam, or, anyway, I don't know her from Eve. We happened to be at the same table at Bustard's, and she threw herself onto me, saying that she had just got to London without money; and I haven't the least idea who she is, or where from, and I don't think she cares tuppence for me, except for any use I can be to her. I gave her two pounds out of charity, and I didn't mean to go beyond that. It was you who talked about putting things down to an account, and now it sounds as though I shall have to pay."

"Only two pounds and nothing beyond that? And I suppose I'm to understand that it's my fault that she's spent more. What about saying you were putting here up for the night? How far did you think forty shillings would go with a girl like her? It's just a case of forty shillings and costs. And costs are about sixty pounds. A lawyer'd say that's about right, wouldn't he? You ought to know."

"Laura, do talk sense. The question is: where did she really come from? She may have had no money yesterday, but what about the week, or the year, before? She wasn't brought to what she is now without someone's cheque book having a good deal to do. I thought you'd find out all about her. It was a woman's work rather than mine. And, of course, not spend anything till you were sure about what you did."

"I should have thought it was a lawyer's work rather than mine. Anyway, it was something I couldn't do. I only learnt that she'd stolen her clothes, and been a dog and a flea, and never told a lie in her life. It's you and I who do that. We scarcely ever stop. And you'll be glad to hear that she's going to get some money from somewhere, and pay the bill. But I won't keep you talking longer. She'll be with you in next to no time. You'd better boil the kettle, and make some tea."

As she said this, she rang off, before he could have time to reply, which she knew would madden him more than anything she could say, even if she'd had more time to think what he wouldn't like it to be.

But Leonard was too occupied with the immediate problem to have much thought, even for her. He knew that his mistake had been in inviting this foreign woman (but was she foreign? He couldn't be sure, even of that) to occupy his friend's rooms, which he had strictly no right to do. Not being aware of her celestial origin, he couldn't console himself with the thought that he had been worsted by forces which a mortal man could not expect to resist successfully, nor would there have been much consolation in that. He was beset by the practical question—even if she should settle down quietly for the night with the many purchases she had made, what was to follow on the next day? He felt convinced that she would not walk out of his life as easily as she had walked in. He wasn't even sure that he would be content for her to do so. That was the core of his trouble. He didn't want her either to walk out or stay in. He wasn't willing to admit to himself that he was disloyal to Laura. He was sure that he loved her as well as ever. But the complication remained. Laura had said that Elya wouldn't object to bigamy. However that might be as a matter of fact, the remark showed that she realised the mess that they were in, and in much the same way that it looked to him. But, under all—or perhaps it should be before all—there was the question of what she was, from where she had come, and what was the background which she must surely have had? If he could get her to tell him that in any sensible, credible way, he might see the way out of the fog in which he was moving now.

And while he was engaged on such thoughts as these, Elya came up the stairs, and entered the room without knocking, which may have been a social custom which she had omitted to learn.

Her arms were laden, and she was followed by a taxi driver who was far more heavily burdened than she. She said gaily: "I can't think why you have stairs. Surely the Earth's large enough for you to all live on the ground. Leonard, you'd better come down with me, and we can bring up the rest. This man feels just as I do about the stairs."

Leonard's thoughts began: "I think you're about the cheekiest bitch...."—but their eyes met, and what he said was: "I shouldn't think there could be much more," and next moment he was following Elya down the stairs, as he had been ordered to do.

He got the remaining boxes out of the vehicle. He searched nearly empty pockets to pay the driver. He led a burdened way up the stairs. He looked back to say: "Hadn't we better take them straight up to your own room?" And was disconcerted by the reply: "No, I want you to see them first, and tell me what I've bought wrong." He said no more, and turned into his own room. Perhaps it would be best to take it all in a casual impersonal way.

Elya was never short of words: she had learnt the language too completely for that. She talked as she unpacked, requiring his opinion on all he saw. He admired hairbrushes. He approved combs. He said that hair nets were undoubtedly all that could be desired. He said that it was the most beautiful dressing gown he had ever seen, which was literally true. Yes, he had no doubt it was very beautiful soap. "I had to stop the taxi," she explained, "and get that from another shop."

"Oh, and this is what I really want to ask you," she said at last. "It's between the transparent and the opaque. I want to know what I'd better wear for the night."

She produced primrose pyjamas, and a nightgown, faintly rose-coloured, which could have been crushed in one hand. She said: "It's queer that people wear things you can see through when there's no one there, and thick things in the day. Or perhaps," she added more thoughtfully, "perhaps it isn't. Perhaps I ought to wear these if I stay upstairs, and that if I come down to you."

"It wouldn't be any good if you did. I always lock up at night."

"You mean you ought to come up to me? I ought to have thought of that."

"No. I wasn't thinking of that."

"Well, it doesn't matter. We can see how they look now."

As she spoke, she began to loosen her clothes. He said hastily: "No, please don't. You really mustn't do that here. Anyone might come in."

She gave him an astonished, outraged glance, such as he had never seen in her eyes before. She said: "Can't you ever tell the truth? As though you couldn't lock the door! Don't you want to see what I'm like? It's about the vilest, rudest thing you could possibly say."

"I didn't mean to be rude," he replied awkwardly, "it's just that you come from a country where they have different customs. It's not usual here."

"I believe," she said, with recovered equanimity, "you could tell lies in your sleep. But there's something else I want to ask you. I want to get hold of some money. What's the best way to do that?"

"It depends upon your qualifications. You'd better tell me what you did before you came here, and then I might be able to help."

Elya, as we know, when she had some clear purpose, was by no means a fool. She suppressed the first reply which came to her mind, and said, with literal truth: "The last thing I did was to learn languages. I think I told you about that before."

"You told me that you knew Chinese and Spanish and French and Russian. If you really know them half as well as you do English, you might make money by teaching them, if you care to do so."

"Half as well? I don't know what you mean. I just know them."

"You may think you do, but it isn't likely that you know them all equally well. Indeed, it isn't a possible thing. You couldn't speak English as you do unless you'd been among English-speaking people for a long while."

"You're quite sure of that? Then I won't tell you it isn't true. But you've got to believe that I know the other languages just the same, or how can you tell me what it's best for me to do?"

"Then we'll agree about that; and if you mislead me you mustn't blame me for anything that goes wrong. But if you've got an ordinary knowledge of all the languages you mention, you might get a fairly high salary as a teacher at a school of languages. If you know any of them, or at least Chinese or Russian, as thoroughly as you know English, you might make a good deal more by giving private tuition."

"Very well, then. I'll do that."

"You'd have to be prepared to tell a straightforward tale as to how you learnt them to that extent, or you might not be believed."

"You mean I've got to make something up? I should think you could help me to do that. Or perhaps Laura would be better than you. I don't want to be rude, but you must know which of you's the better at a good lie."

"But I shouldn't advise you to do that. You might get into serious trouble. Why not tell the truth for a change?"

"Because, if you don't believe me, it's not likely that anyone else would."

"We won't go over all that again. There's a sixty pound bill to be paid, and if you're serious about this I'll give you the best help I can. My father happens to be in the Foreign Office, and if you like to come down to Godalming with me, he may know of someone—say someone who's got an appointment in the Diplomatic Service—who'd pay well for some good coaching in the language he's got to talk in a month's time."

"I expect that's a good plan. Is it far to go?"

"We can get there in an hour or two by rail; and, if you like, we'll come back by car."

"Yes, I should. And if I pay all the sixty pounds, may I show you how I look in the nightgown when I've done that?"

"Perhaps we'd better talk about that when the time comes," he answered weakly.

"You know you're just putting it off. Suppose Laura does it as well? Will that make it all right?"

"You'd better ask Laura what she thinks about that."

"So I will. When we're in the train."

"You think Laura's coming to Godalming?"

"She wouldn't like being left behind."

Leonard thought Elya might be right about that.

CHAPTER EIGHT

LIVELINESS AT GODALMING

Elya went upstairs at last, and Leonard decided to ring Laura up (as was a nightly custom) and inform her of what had happened and been arranged.

He told her almost literally everything which had been said, which gave some measure of relief to an anxious mind. His only deliberate omission was Elya's suggestion that Laura might like to exhibit herself for competition in a rival nightgown. He hoped that there was no disloyalty to her in recognising that it was not a contest she would have been likely to win; and that the idea of it would not be gladly received.

He felt that all was well till he came to the projected Godalming expedition, when he got a cold retort: "I can't see why you can't enquire without taking her there."

But he had an answer to that. "You see, Laura, the Governor knows more than a bit about one or two of those languages himself, and I want him to make sure that she won't let us down. You know what a liar she is, and it isn't sense to suppose she knows them all equally well. I shouldn't have risked it at all if I hadn't been so anxious to get hold of the sixty pounds. Oh, by the way, she asked if you could come along."

"She did *what*?"

"Asked if you could come."

"I wonder what she's up to now. Yes, I think I will."

"Then what about the ten-forty-five tomorrow? Gets us in comfortably before lunch."

"That'll suit me, dear. Wonder if she'll say she's never been in a train before."

"I shouldn't think she'd be quite such a fool as that."

"Then she hasn't said as much to you as she did to me."

The conversation ended at that, and Leonard got into bed (as he had been ready to do), and was up early enough next morning to be dressed when Elya rattled the knob of a locked door.

"Slept well?" he asked politely, as she came in, radiantly calm, and bringing a perfume she had shown him the night before.

"Yes, I did. Isn't it a queer thing? And now I know what a dream's like. I dreamed I was back where I belong, and it made me see what a fool I am."

"I don't think I should call you that. But I might understand you better if you said where it really was."

"Suppose we talk about breakfast instead."

"A Mrs. Hawkins will be here in about twenty minutes. She gets breakfast for me, and puts the place straight."

"I suppose you've got plenty for two?"

"Possibly. But don't you think it will look better if you have it in your own room?"

"No, I don't. Wouldn't it look as though we'd quarrelled if anyone thought about it? But why should they? There isn't any law against it, is there?"

"No, it isn't illegal."

"I suppose you know all the laws?"

"No. Nobody could."

"Then how can you tell that there isn't one about having breakfast?"

"Because it would be too absurd."

"Which must mean that it's not the wrong thing to do. I suppose you have so many laws so no one can know them all, and they keep getting broken, and you get money for that?"

"It isn't quite that simple, but it works out that way often enough."

"I should think it must. What do you do while Mrs. Hawkins is cleaning the room? You must swallow a lot of dust."

"What made you think of that?"

"I'm always thinking of things. I think of lots that I don't say. I just like to know."

"I sit here while she gets breakfast in the kitchen. She's in there, or doing my bedroom, while I have breakfast, and then I go into the bedroom while she's in here."

"Well, I can do the same. I only hope she won't be long. I've been hungry all the time since I came here."

"Did you get more to eat in your own country?"

"It was different. We ate like pigs. I know that's the right thing to say, but I don't know what it means. How do pigs eat? Not that it matters. We ate all we could get inside us when a star—but you wouldn't understand that. You'd say that we ate about twice a year. I'm glad I've not got to wait now. I think Mrs. Hawkins is coming up."

This proved to be right, and the lady mentioned, entering next moment, would have retired on seeing one whom she supposed to be a client occupying the room, but on Leonard saying hastily: "Mrs. Hawkins, this is a lady who's using Mr. Bentley's room while he's away. I've asked her to have breakfast with me, as I didn't suppose she'd find much left there. Can you scrape up enough for two?"

Mrs. Hawkins, a small spare woman, lifted her head, pushed back some wisps of sandy-grey hair from her forehead, and gazed intently upon the angelic vision. She said: "Well I shalln't tell him. I'm always a good sport," and finding that this remark was received in silence, she had no doubt that she had understood and accepted the position in a wisely tolerant way. She added that there would be plenty for two, which Elya was glad to hear.

But she soon heard that there was to be a time limit to what she ate, for Leonard said that he must visit his bank to get the money which would be required for the train journey, and other purposes, which led to a number of curiously elementary and yet penetrating questions regarding the nature, functions, and management of banks, during which Leonard admitted a doubt which had been on the threshold of his mind more than once before. Was it possible that Elya's professed ignorance was something more— or less—than a pose? If it were not genuine, it was so detailed, so elaborate a pretence. Accustomed to cross-examine, and judge veracity, he recognised that she was consistent in all she said, and had a convincing aspect of a candour—only excepting the fantastic foundation on which she built. Had he erred in too ready assumption that this foundation was no more than a blatant lie? He resolved to ask his father's opinion, being a judgement on which he had learnt that he could very safely rely.

They took a taxi to the bank, and then went straight on to Victoria station. Elya said it was all new to her, which her continual curiosity supported, but her coolness made hard to believe. They arrived without incident, and Leonard having telephoned before starting, they were met by one of his father's cars.

They drove through a picturesque village, to a country manor which stood in its own well-wooded grounds, and were welcomed pleasantly by Sir Andrew Weyleigh, a man as dark and lean, but somewhat taller than his son, and looking ten years younger than the fifty-nine during which he had endured, with gentlemanly toleration, the trouble of mortal life.

He was a widower, without other children than Leonard, and his sole interest in life, when away from Downing Street, was in his garden and home. He was now taking a summer vacation in the way that he preferred, by spending it in his own grounds. He was glad to welcome his son and any friends whom he might bring, especially Laura, she being a choice he approved.

Laura took Elya up to a room which she used when visiting there, and which was called hers, while Leonard, joining his father in the library below, took the opportunity to explain something of the strange woman who, in the last twenty-four hours, had fixed herself so firmly upon him.

"It sounds," Sir Andrew said, "as though it's your fault for having offered to put her up, which you'd no business to do. I shouldn't have thought that any girl could have put it across you as slick as that. She ought to be worth seeing. But as to the languages, she's stringing you along more likely than not, and that's where I may be able to give you a leg up."

After that, they went in to lunch, and as he seated Elya at his right hand, he had his own moment of wonder, not that Leonard had been subdued, but that the serenity of her eyes could conceal the adventuress which he had confidently assumed her to be.

He resolved to keep the talk to indifferent topics until the meal should be at its concluding stages, seeing the awkwardness which must result if he should convict their guest of deceit at an earlier time, but he found that it was not easy to do. Any subject might excite Elya's lively curiosity, and then expose ignorance—if it were genuine—abysmal and unashamed.

And then, when the talk wandered to the cultivation of his one two-acre arable field, she broke into the conversation with the exclamation: "Oh, I learnt all about that!"—and showed a knowledge of artificial manures far surpassing his own.

When he felt the time had come for the language test, he said: "I am told that you know Spanish thoroughly?" And when she said yes to this, he addressed her at once in Russian, and was answered at equal speed in the same tongue.

Recognising that this trap had failed, and being unable to test her in the Asian tongue, he asked, with increased respect: "You know Chinese equally?"

"Yes. I just know it."

"And you can write it also?"

"Yes. I learnt that at the same time."

"Do you mind telling me where and when?"

"I don't mind. But I can't get anyone to believe."

"Have you tried many times?"

"No. I only began yesterday. I see what you mean. I might find others have got more sense."

"Yes. I might have worded it differently, but I meant that. I think that I might believe, if you should tell me a true tale. Will you do that?"

"Yes, of course. I was an angel till yesterday. Then I came here to have a look round. I like being a girl best, but I can be other things if I choose. I've been a dog and a flea."

"Would you mind being one or other again for a few minutes, so that no one could disbelieve?"

"I'd rather be something else for a change."

"That sounds fair enough. Within limits, of course. It wouldn't do to be a bad-tempered tiger; and an elephant might be bad for the chairs."

"Yes. I see that. Perhaps I'd better go on being a flea. But I don't want to get crushed. I'd soon show you, if you could guarantee that."

"It is a most reasonable stipulation. Suppose we say this: I will lay my hand, palm down, on the table, and you shall get on it, and give it two bites. I will keep my other hand down, and all the others will do the same. Would that give you time to change back if you should be frightened, or only enough for a good jump?"

"That would be safe enough. I should have lots of time to change back before I could get hit."

"Then that's how it shall be, and we shall all be grateful if you'll show us what you can do."

As he spoke, he laid his clenched hand, knuckles upward, upon the table, from which all other hands disappeared, and next moment the fascinated spectators, including a butler behind his chair, saw her clothes collapse in emptiness on her seat, and then slip sideways on to the floor. Then, on the back of Sir Andrew's hand, there was the small brown body for which they looked. The hand remained motionless while the tiny body swelled with the blood it drew. Then it hopped an inch, gave a brief nip, and was gone.

All eyes were turned from the bitten hand to the empty chair, expecting, half fearfully, that the sagging clothes would be rounded again by an inward form. But nothing happened. Elya had gone; but did she mean to return? It seemed that the visiting angel had withdrawn contemptuously from an incredulous world. Leonard was aware of a sharp regret; and even Laura felt that she would have chosen a different end.

CHAPTER NINE

ELYA HAS HER OWN WAY

For some minutes the three who remained seated round the table gazed silently at the empty chair. Then they were conscious of a scuffling movement beneath them, at which the butler stooped down to look under the table. Was it Elya about to show herself in a new form?

But Beddoes gave a different explanation. "I'm afraid, sir," he said, "the cat's got into the room."

He opened the door to eject an animal to which he knew his master had a nervous antipathy, and they soon saw a black streak darting through it.

"Didn't it," Laura asked, "have something—perhaps a mouse—in its mouth?"

Leonard said: "No, it was larger than that. More like a young rat."

"You don't think Elya could have made some mistake, and got caught?"

"She's always seemed very well able to take care of herself," he answered, with more confidence in the words than the tone in which they were spoken.

His father asked: "Aren't you taking it a bit too seriously? I should call it the cleverest conjuring trick that I ever saw."

"I don't know what to believe," his son answered doubtfully. "The flea-bites look real enough."

Sir Andrew admitted that, in a fair but still sceptical mind. He said the language claim had seemed to be genuine too. "But I expect she's laughing at how she's tricked us, and you won't be much older before you'll see her again, and I only hope she'll tell us how it was done."

He was right on one point at least, for as he spoke she entered the room.

She came in serenely, in the form which it may be convenient to regard as that of her real self, and exhibiting its slender well-rounded loveliness in the rose-coloured transparency about which she had been so annoyingly thwarted before. She walked past the astonished butler to her own seat, from which she pushed the clothes which were not already upon the floor, and looked round with the smile of triumph appropriate to the event.

"I think," she said complaisantly, "I've done rather well. When I found how sharp my teeth were, I was dreadfully afraid of getting it torn."

"You are asking us to believe," Sir Andrew queried sceptically, "that you were the cat that ran out of the room?"

"Yes, of course. I should have thought anyone would have seen that. If I hadn't gone out of the room, how could I have come back?"

There was a simple logic about this argument which even Sir Andrew felt to be too strong to attack. He said:

"Well, perhaps it will save trouble if we agree to take it all in, till you deal us the cards in another way. But don't you think you would be warmer in your clothes than as you are now?"

"I don't mind either way now. But Leonard was so rude that I made up my mind not to let him off. I think he's annoyed that Laura's figure isn't equal to mine."

"I don't know anything about Leonard being rude," Sir Andrew replied firmly, "but someone is certainly being rude now. We all know that Laura has an excellent figure, and you must forgive me saying that she will make him a much better wife than you would be likely to do."

"I don't see how we could settle that, unless we both try. Three months each might be about right, and Laura can say whether she'll take the first turn. You can't want anything fairer than that."

"I think you may find that Leonard's choice is already made, and on a more permanent basis than you forecast. But as we are all finished, I propose that we shall withdraw, and leave you here to resume your clothes. Beddoes, the clearing of the table must be deferred."

He turned to Elya again as he rose, to say: "We are retiring to the library, where you will doubtless join us when you are ready. The door is slightly to the left, on the other side of the hall."

A minute later he was saying: "She's the cleverest conjurer that I ever saw. I can't even guess how it was done. But the less you see of her the better. You've had twenty-four hours now, and if you live a hundred years I don't suppose you'll want any more. A woman without the most elementary decency—! If she thinks I'm going to recommend her to any friend of mine after that exhibition, she'll find she's made a bad guess."

"Oh, but, Sir Andrew," Laura exclaimed in dismay, "don't you see what a hole we shall be in if you don't? You're forgetting my sixty pounds."

"I'd rather pay it myself. I'm not going to recommend a woman who's liable to get out of her clothes any moment she feels like it. There might be such a scandal that I should have to resign."

Leonard said: "I don't think there'd be any danger of that. It would be too difficult to believe. But don't you think we might get her to promise to behave properly? She says she never told a lie in her life."

"Which is the biggest one anyone can possibly tell. I'll tell you how far I'm prepared to go, though it's against my own judgement, and—" But whatever he might have said they were not destined to hear, for at that moment Elya entered the room.

She gave Sir Andrew a dazzling smile, and addressed him with her usual directness.

"I suppose you think I look better now I've got back into the clothes. It's about the best joke that I ever heard. But it was a very nice lunch, though I could have eaten rather more than I had. Leonard said he didn't want to be late back, so perhaps you'd better tell me now whom I'm to teach, and how much money I'm to get."

"I've been thinking that, with your exceptional qualifications, you might do better by opening a language school. You could advertise at first, and you'd soon have such testimonials that—"

"Do you think that, being a foreigner she'd be allowed—?" Leonard interposed, seeing it from the legal angle, as he was likely to do.

"Yes, it's not like acting. They let foreigners teach their own gabble."

"But she might have to prove her nationality, and produce her papers."

"It's not a matter which is dealt with in my department. It's a Home Office affair; but that sounds likely enough. There shouldn't be any difficulty about it. She'd have to stop playacting with them."

"Suppose she really hasn't got any."

"That's absurd. How would she have landed here? Unless, of course, she's English, in which case we're worrying about nothing."

"I've told you I'm an angel," Elya interposed. "You tell so many lies yourselves that you never believe anything. I know what you mean by papers, and of course I haven't got any. But I don't want to open a school. I'd rather take on one at a time, and finish teaching him first. I thought of two hundred pounds for one language, or twice as much for a stupid man."

But this simple method of charging roused a chorus of criticism.

Laura said: "I don't think you'd get anyone to pay that."

"If he said he hadn't finished learning," Leonard objected, "you might have to go on forever."

"If you put it that way," Sir Andrew prophesied, "you wouldn't have much chance of being offered a higher fee."

"You can tell me the best way to charge," she agreed readily. "But I'm not going to start a school. What I'd really like is a man who makes laws, and while I taught him I could tell him a few to try. I might do a lot of good."

"If I advise you," Sir Andrew began, "that a school would be best—"

"I've told you I don't *want* a school," she interrupted, in the tone of one who was being patient with a difficult child, "I think you're trying to get out of what you were going to do, and if that's it, I should like to know why."

Leonard said: "I don't think my father has any doubt that you could teach the languages, but he may wonder whether you'd do or say anything else."

"You mean turning into something I shouldn't be? But why should I? I had to before I could get the clothes that you fuss about all the time. I shouldn't have done it just now if I hadn't been asked, so it isn't sense to complain about that. I shall not do anything of the kind."

"Perhaps, if you promise that…," Sir Andrew began, but was interrupted by: "I wasn't promising. I was just telling the truth."

He paused to consider this, and then said: "It is a narrow distinction, but very real. You may be surprised to know that it gives me more confidence than I was feeling before. I will do this. I will give you letters of introduction to the Chinese and Russian Embassies, and if they tell me that you know their languages as thoroughly as I am disposed to believe, I think, between us, we shall be able to find you something to do; and I shall rely on you not to play any conjuring tricks that would let me down."

CHAPTER TEN

ELYA MAKES PLANS

When lunch was over, Leonard asked his father for the loan of one of the cars, and was surprised by a momentary hesitation, which he had not expected. "The fact is," he added, "I promised to give Elya a ride back to town whenever I brought her here."

"The fact is," Sir Andrew answered, "I may want to send the Bentley in for an overhaul any day now, but I wouldn't refuse you the other because of that. What I wish is that you'd got another reason for wanting it. You've only known your angel, if that's what we're to call her (but how do you know that she hasn't come from the other place?), for about twenty-four hours, and you seem to have got over a good deal of ground in that time, in more senses than one. But if you've promised, I don't want to let you down. She evidently knows what a car is. I shouldn't have been surprised if she'd said that she never saw one in her life before."

"That was just what she did. But she saw them when she looked out of Bustard's window. She said she thought everyone must be mad, and if there were an accident they all ought to be taken off the road at once."

"And then she wants to get into one herself on the next day? Well that's how we mostly are. There are lots of us who eat mutton and wouldn't be willing to kill a sheep. The girls ought to be ready in half an hour. (I wonder what she talks about when she gets Laura alone). I'll tell Reeves to have the Morris ready for you by then."

The girls were not ready in half an hour. It was more than that. But the time came when Elya shook hands with her host with a charming smile, ("I think you've been kinder than I deserved."), and surveyed the Morris saloon with approving, but yet questioning eyes.

Then she turned to Leonard to say: "I suppose Laura can drive, and we'd better sit in the back."

"No. I prefer to do my own driving."

"It won't be much fun sitting in front while you're doing that."

"We can agree there. You'd better sit in the back with Laura. I like to concentrate on the road."

"Yes. You ought to. You might run over a dog. I shouldn't like that. I should think that it might have been me."

She appeared oblivious of the curtness with which the offer of her society had been rebuffed, and went on serenely: "I don't mind if Laura isn't with you. I like talking to her. She knows lots of things that I don't, and she's better tempered now she's going to get paid, and I'm going to see other men, and not only you. I've told her it's about over for you; and I expect Sir Andrew was right about her making a good wife. She can't help being a bad shape.

You ought always to think of that. I should say you'd better kiss in the dark." She became aware that Laura was standing beside her, and turned to her without embarrassment. "Laura, I've been telling Leonard how to manage when you get married, so that he won't be thinking of me. I'm getting into the back with you."

The next hour was spent in discussion of the amenities of the home they had just left, which Elya approved. She showed a detailed exactness in memory of what she had seen, which she contrasted with the comparative austerities of the chambers in which she had spent the previous night. She expressed a resolve that she would charge sufficient for the language lessons to enable her to live in the same style.

Laura said: "You didn't act as though anything had been new to you."

"I didn't say that it was. I'd learnt about it, but seeing's quite different. I mean to have a coal fire, and a bearskin rug."

"Well, I should think you might manage that, even without vamping anyone more than it seems natural for you to do."

"I don't vamp anyone," Elya replied equably. "What misleads you is that I'm always natural and sincere. You don't understand my doing what you don't practise yourselves. But as for Leonard, who seems to be the only man in the world for you (which seems queer, when you look at how full of men the streets are), you'll like to know that I've no more use for him, and I think that he feels the same about me. But I've told you that, or something like it, a few minutes ago."

Laura gave her no thanks for this assurance. She may have felt that none was due, even though she had believed more than she did. She asked bluntly: "What are you going to do tonight?"

"I'm going back to my room, unless Leonard gets sulky and locks me out. Or I suppose, as you're Mr. Bentley's sister, you could do that. But I expect to get somewhere else tomorrow."

Laura made no comment on that. She didn't see how it was to be done, but she certainly didn't intend to be the one to propose difficulties. She thought even one more night of propinquity would be more than she wished Leonard to have; especially as she had an engagement for the evening which it would be difficult to break. But that also was best unmentioned.

Yet she need not have vexed her mind. Elya, with the sincerity she professed, had said exactly what she intended to do. Although she and Leonard had a meal together before returning to his chambers, he found her to be as impersonally distant as at their first encounter. She was not cold, but neutral, in an atmosphere which most women would have found hard to sustain, but which was easy to her.

She withdrew at an early hour to the solitude of Mr. Bentley's bed, but she was not quick to sleep. She lay awake for some hours, and was quite unworried by that. Indeed, on the previous night, she had been puzzled and warily cautious of the hiatus of sleep and dreams which she knew to be natural to her adopted existence; but experience is a different matter.

Men abandon consciousness as a routine event. The idea of unsleeping life would seem to many of them to be an abnormal or impossible thing. Yet sleep is not a necessity of recuperation, even to the creatures of Earth. Many birds sleep much through the dark months, but little, if at all, in the summer nights. Many creatures, such as sharks, do not sleep at all.

Elya saw that, while she elected to be a woman, her body must behave as a woman's does; but she did not fret at her wakeful hours.

In the quietude of the night, she reviewed her two days of humanity, and decided that she had made a good start. She thought that she was going to have—and had had already—a most enjoyable time. But it remained that the day's events were no more than an episode that she intended to leave behind. She had done with Leonard. She was not sure how he felt about her. But Laura could have him. Now that she was a woman, she found that she was longing for men. Probably it was inevitable. Anyway it was likely to be good fun.

But she did not want Leonard now. She probably never would have given him two amorous thoughts if he had not first thrust himself upon her, and then pretended that he didn't want to see her properly, so that his insincerity had roused her disgust, and his rudeness had stirred her ire. But Laura must do for him. She would be engaged in the stalking of higher game.

She was resolved that the next day should not pass without her acquiring a home of her own, and considered how this could be done. She had a wide knowledge of the life around her, and the routines that it required. She had supposed this to be comprehensive, until she had learnt that its innumerable details were incomplete, and that it was practised in bewilderingly illogical ways. She must review each step in advance, lest she stumble to her own discomfiture.

There was this silly question of names. She knew that if she applied for a flat or house and said that her name was Elya, they would require additions, in the absence of which she would almost certainly be rebuffed. What should she do about that? In the regions from which she came, everyone had had one name, neither more nor less, which was the sensible way. Or, at least— She was fair enough to recognise one of the differences arising from the fact that these people had only temporary existences. They must distinguish ancestry and children from themselves. Anyway, a surname was a necessity here. What could be done? The impish humour which had betrayed her to censure in the heavenly courts proposed an audacity beyond anything she had yet done. She had suggested Fitz-Gabriel once before, but seen that Leonard thought that there was something wrong about that. What about Gabriel? Miss Elya Gabriel had a satisfactory sound. As to what Gabriel would say when it should come to his knowledge, as it was almost certain to do, even her lively imagination could not conceive. But it would be a past event, and even an archangel could not alter that! Miss Elya Gabriel it should be.

Then there was the question of references. Even though she should have money (which was not yet in her bag), she knew that they were likely to be required.

She thought first of Leonard, with a rather narrow, scrupulous mind. He would be likely to write in a cautious way, which might be misunderstood—or perhaps understood would be the more accurate word. What about Laura? She had learnt that Miss Bentley lived with her mother, who was of the highest respectability. Laura *wanted* her to leave. And she was a woman. If she wanted anything, she wouldn't let a little matter, such as writing a reference, block the way. And then how furious she would be!

The thought of Laura's fury settled the matter. Laura it should most certainly be. But for a second? Inspiration came. Leonard's father had a sense of humour. And (although he ought not to have talked about conjuring tricks) he had understood her far better than any other inhabitant of this planet whom she had met. Then he was already committed to getting her some teaching engagements. Could he do this, and deny that she was fitted to rent a home? And she felt that he might actually enjoy being used in that audacious manner. The thought of his appreciation was as potent as that of Laura's fury in deciding that it should be.

Having arranged these matters to her satisfaction, she went to sleep with a quiet mind.

CHAPTER ELEVEN

ELYA HAS A FULL DAY

Mrs. Hawkins had finished laying the breakfast, and Leonard was wondering whether he should start by himself, or send her up to announce it, before Elya appeared, and then it was in a dressing gown which may have had something underneath it, but not much.

She said: "I'm later than I was yesterday, but I went on sleeping. It doesn't matter to me, because I can't go out till your father telephones to say what he's fixed up; but I shall have lots to do after that."

"I hope you won't want to be here after ten. I've got to be in court by ten-thirty, and I shall need to have a short conference before that."

"You mean you wouldn't like leaving me here?"

"I mean it would be awkward about locking up."

"Then why not leave it unlocked? No one would be likely to come. Nobody'd know."

"I should not care to do that."

"Then I shall have to be a flea again, and get through the key-hole. I'd meant to give that kind of thing up, because everyone seems to think it's a bit queer."

"I wouldn't say bit's the word. But I don't think it would do, even if you could really manage that way. What about your clothes?"

"That's easy. I should take them off first, and put them outside the door."

"You mean you'd dress on the stairs?"

"Yes. Why not?"

"Someone might come up."

"They'd get over it quite easily, if they did."

"Well, it wouldn't do."

"Then I could carry them up, and dress in my own room."

"We shall have to think of something better than that."

"Then I'll bring you the key in court. I should like that. If you shouldn't be sure what the law is, I might be able to help you with an idea."

"I'm afraid that wouldn't be any use. If I can't persuade the judge what the law is, he'll settle it in his own way. He wouldn't listen to you."

"Oh, he would, if I spoke loud. I can promise you that. I've noticed people do listen to me."

"Well, I'd much rather you don't come. I think we shall have to leave together. You must telephone my father from somewhere else."

"I'm not going to do that without any reason at all. I can bring my things down here before you go, and lock up that room, and give you the key, and then I can lock this when I go out, and put the key through the door, and you can get it when you come back."

"Yes. I suppose that will do."

"You needn't say it in that tone. Of course it will. If you can't think out little things like that, it's no wonder the laws get muddled."

"Actually, I don't make the laws."

"No. I expect you just tangle them up."

"You're not being very polite this morning."

"I didn't mean to be rude. I was just thinking aloud. You've been very nice to me. And I've got to ask you to lend me another pound. I shall pay them all back tonight."

"Yes, I can do that."

The note changed hands, and as breakfast was now finished, Elya went up to her own room at once, and came down dressed for the street, and with the key in her hand.

Leonard went, and she waited idly until the telephone rang. She picked it up, with the thought: "Why do men have these clumsy wires? But it wouldn't be any use to say anything." And then: "Yes, Sir Andrew, Elya speaking. Oh, you are a dear! I knew you'd do it. Yes, of course I understand that. No, if you tell me the addresses, I shan't forget. Why should I? There's no need to write them down. Yes, there'll be lots of time. I'm glad it's not later. I've got to find a home for myself after lunch. Laura's giving me a reference. And I'm using your name as well. I shouldn't have mentioned that except that you'll have to know that I've got two names. I'm Elya Gabriel. You know that I couldn't get anything without that. I don't believe you're a bit pleased. I thought you'd do more for Laura than that. Well, it is. She wants me to get away from Leonard. And I know there's a law about sleeping all night in the streets. I don't suppose anyone knows why. But how could I go on teaching Chinese while I was in jail for that?

Well, if it were a fine? I don't suppose Laura would find the money. And I'm sure Leonard doesn't want to find any more. You must see that a reference is the best way."

"You are a very enterprising young woman. I daresay I can say something for you, if you'll promise me that you won't do anything freakish. But if you told me the truth yesterday, when you said that you could turn into a flea, I don't see why you couldn't get out of jail without troubling Leonard."

"But I should have thought that anyone could see that! I couldn't carry all my clothes about on a flea's back. And think how far I might have to hop to get back to Leonard. And if I jumped on anyone, he might be going the wrong way."

"They are most logical arguments. But we'd better stop talking, or you'll be late for your first appointment."

"Yes, I needn't have said all that. But you do have such wild ideas. I'll let you know how I get on."

But Sir Andrew did not wait to have a report from her. He was sufficiently curious to ring up the Chinese Embassy after lunch. He expected only to speak to one of the secretaries, but was put through to the ambassador, who wished to thank him personally for the celestial presence who had been directed to him. He had satisfied himself that Elya had never been in China. It was common sense that no English woman could have acquired a knowledge of the language so complete and idiomatic without prolonged residence there—and most improbable, even then. He always believed in accepting the simplest and most probable explanation. He had no doubt that Elya came from the skies.

Recognising that a perfect teacher requires the fullest knowledge of both languages concerned, and being satisfied that her command of English was equal to that of his own tongue, he had engaged her to give advanced lessons in the latter language to some of his own staff. Naturally, she had required to be highly paid. There was a faint, though very courteous, hint that there might even have been a little difficulty about that. Her request for a substantial sum in advance had also been a little unusual. But lack of mundane experience may both explain and excuse. He had given her fifteen pounds.

Satisfied of the success of this recommendation, Sir Andrew then rang up the Russian Embassy. Here a voice which was certainly not that of the ambassador seemed more desirous of obtaining information than handing it out.

Yes, the lady had called. She had admitted that she was not English. Could Sir Andrew say what her nationality might be?

"No," he answered cautiously. "I think she has only recently come to this country. But she was reticent as to what her real nationality is, or perhaps I didn't understand her reply."

"Then you're not really in a position to guarantee her in any way?"

"It has been a very short acquaintance. But she said she had exceptional knowledge of Russian, and I was curious to know how far you could confirm this. I don't know it well enough myself to be a good judge."

"Oh, she knows Russian. Like a native, or almost better than that. But she wouldn't admit that she'd ever been there, and that's simply absurd. And her name doesn't tell us much. She might be Polish. She might be Hungarian. She might even be Czech."

"But I take it she won't be much use to you?"

"Oh, I'm not saying that, though I don't see what it would be. I hoped you could have told us more about her. But I know you run up against all sorts, just as we do, and we're obliged to you for letting us have a look. She certainly wouldn't get far with us unless she could be a lot franker than she's been yet. But thanks all the same."

As he finished, he rang off too promptly for Sir Andrew to say more, which he was equally disinclined to do. He saw that it was assumed that he had contacted her in some way through his official position at the F.O., and he saw no reason why that impression should be disturbed. He was not told that Elya had gone away with twenty pounds in her bag, in addition to the fifteen she had had from a friendlier source. But the second amount had not been paid in anticipation of it being earned by proficiency in the Russian tongue. It was given to a foreign woman, who was a clever linguist, who had said plainly that she owed no loyalty to the British Crown, and had expressed political opinions, in response to adroit questioning, which, if not communistic, were certainly not such as a capitalist would approve. It was given in anticipation that she might talk more freely on a later occasion, and so that she should know, if she should have need of money (as most women do), where it could be easily had.

But Sir Andrew had little time to consider this conversation before he was called to the telephone again on Elya's behalf. Messrs Gawthorne, Ellis & Gawthorne, Estate Agents, had been referred to him by a Miss Gabriel, who had enquired of them respecting a small luxury flat at £9.9.0 weekly, which she had now gone to see. Would she be a respectable and responsible tenant? She had been unable to give a bank reference, saying that she had only just come to this country. Sir Andrew judged the speaker to be well impressed by the personality of this lovely applicant, but dubious of the vagueness of her replies to the routine questions which it was natural for them to ask. If he should reply in the same way, it was a poor hope that she would get the flat she desired. He was not a poor man, and he had a whimsical inclination to see what Elya would do on a loose rein. He said: "The lady is just arrived from a distance, but there may be reasons why it would be indiscreet for her to be more explicit than that. I do not think it to be a matter in which I can interfere officially, but I should be quite willing to give you a personal guarantee for a month's rent, if that will be satisfactory."

"That," was the cautious reply, "will be quite satisfactory so far as the rent is concerned, but of course there are other considerations in letting a flat of this character. The point is that she wants to get into it this afternoon, and if she's to do that, we ought to have an agreement ready when she gets back."

"You mean if she's prepared to take it after the inspection?"

"I don't think," Mr. Ellis answered, rather coldly, "that there'll be much doubt of that. Sir Henry Wilton had it till last week."

"Well, she won't be likely to steal the spoons, if you mean that, or put fleas into the bed."

He was conscious, even as he spoke, that he might have illustrated his meaning in better ways, but Mr. Ellis could have no suspicion of that. He said: "I didn't suppose anything of the kind. But with a lady who's on her own— well, I'm certain you'll understand that we like to be sure who our tenants are."

"Yes. I appreciate that. But I really don't think you need have any doubt."

Mr. Ellis thanked him, and rang off. It had occurred to him that, in view of Sir Andrew's position at the Foreign Office, there might be diplomatic reasons for accommodating a mysterious foreign visitor which he might not be willing to explain in a telephone conversation. That would account for the offer to guarantee the rent. Or it would be equally explicable if she were one in whom he were taking a more personal interest. Well, if there should be discretion, such as might be anticipated from one in his position—it might be best not to probe further. He said he thought that would be all that it would be necessary to ask. Should the lady decide to take it, he would write by that night's post, enclosing the form of the guarantee.

When Elya got back, she found that the agreement awaited her signature, and if Mr. Ellis took the extra precaution of asking her for a week's rent in advance, well, as the guarantee was still unsigned, he could hardly be blamed for that. It was a condition which met with smiling assent, and as she gave him a sight of the bank notes her bag contained, he concluded that all was well.

CHAPTER TWELVE

IN WHICH NOTHING HAPPENS

Elya lay in the bed which Sir Henry Wilton had not despised, and was well content. She felt that she had secured herself in a position which even Gabriel could not contemn. Last evening she had had the satisfaction of removing her possessions from Mr. Bentley's inferior chambers, and of telling Leonard of the day's successes. Now she looked forward to exploiting the openings which she had made. The teaching of languages was not an end in itself. It would be rather a bore; and she had not come here to be bored, but to have some fun, and so she meant it to be.

The serenity of her mind was not agitated by vain regrets, but she recognised that she had bypassed an attractive possibility in not having gone to the law courts with Leonard, and perhaps having a few words with those who dispensed the too-numerous laws, which no one man was equal to understand. There *must* be comic possibilities there. Tragic ones too, she had wit to see, but she had a buoyancy of mind which could not easily be ruffled by troubles which were not hers. And if they were such a pest, why did not these half-wit humans sweep them away?

She thought too, with satisfaction, of the fact that she was not bound to stay in London, or elsewhere in England, if the application of her lively logic to the comic antics of the humans round her should be unsatisfactory in its results. The languages which she had acquired gave her the freedom of nine-tenths of the inhabited surface of the terrestrial globe.

But there was one basic question to be resolved. She had the power of transformation, as she had abundantly proved. She was a young woman now. She had been a dog. She had been a flea. (Or would several fleas be more exact?) For a brief minute she had been a cat. And through all these metamorphoses she had been herself, as she was now.

That was true, but she knew that it oversimplified what occurred. Blended with her own nature, in every instance, had been that of the incarnation she had achieved.

As a dog, she had felt the impulse to guard property from a thieving hand, even though it been that of strangers who had no claim of loyalty on herself. She had had an inclination to use her teeth on the legs of men.

As a flea, she had felt a fierce joy as she distended her body with human blood. She had even enjoyed foiling the pursuit of clumsy hands with enormous leaps. She had been fearless, sure of herself, contemptuous of pursuit, even while her own overruling reason had insisted that it was a peril she must avoid.

As a cat, she had been wary and swift. She had been cunningly silent while securing the cobweb garment from the pocket of the dressing gown which had trailed from the chair; furtively swift as she had borne it in her mouth from the room. It had seemed natural to her then to carry anything in her mouth. It had been the obvious thing to do—and to do so carefully that even that delicate fabric had not been torn. (Must not a kitten be carried at times in the same way?)

And now that she was a girl she had a girl's passions and impulses, and even some of a girl's restraints. There was exciting novelty here. But was it worth being experienced to the full?

She would not have liked to settle down as a dog. Nor as a cat. Nor even as a flea, though it would always be a merriment to recall. They had been experiences to welcome, but not prolong. Should she take her present form in an equally casual way? Should she continue to sample the physical bodies of mundane life in momentary promiscuous forms? Or should she continue to develop the one she had now contrived?

On the whole—unless she should be caught in an exceptionally slimy pit—she thought that she would continue to play the game in her present form, though it might be to an end which she could not guess.

Having come to this resolution, she turned her thoughts to the engagements which she had made. She had a definite appointment with the Chinese Embassy for the next day. That was a pleasant and simple matter, for those whom she had met there had seemed to be harmless, and almost sane.

The less definite appointment was with those whom she had judged to be of a more sinister sort.

From one or both of these openings she would doubt-less be able to explore further into the fascinating lunacies of the world around her, and in this happy confidence she lapsed into the peaceful sleep which only those of good health and good conscience know.

It was eight next morning when she came out of the bathroom, yawning luxuriously. She threw off her dressing gown, and faced the mirror, a vision of perfect nudity which would have reduced the Medician Venus to the status of a back-street urchin of no account.

She looked with happy approval at what she saw, but her thoughts were on other things. She must cease to be Elya to all she met. She was Miss Gabriel now. Teacher of languages. And what an expert she was!

The impish humour which she had retired to the back-most corner of her mind, and which she thought she had locked away, kicked the panels of its confinement, and chuckled with anticipatory glee. Her knowledge of Chinese was *complete*. There was no gutter-slang, no jargon of vice or crime, no indecency that she did not know. Suppose she should use a selection from this repertory at the Embassy, casually, jestingly, or in a smiling intimate way? Or with flippant impudence? Or as though innocently unconscious of the implications of what she said?

Choice examples came to a dancing mind.

Or suppose she should teach them so that they should be used blindly at ceremonial moments by those who believed their meaning to be other than that it was? So that one who would think himself to be saying: *Humbly I kiss your celestial hand* would actually say—but there is no need to translate that, even though it could be precisely done. She was thinking in Chinese, which has some extremities of language different from ours.

But she rebuked herself for this thought, which she put away. It would be dishonourable to mislead so largely. The cupboard should remain locked, though its occupant might be kicking hard. She was Miss Gabriel now.

CHAPTER THIRTEEN

EMBASSIES DIFFER

It is pleasant to be believed, pleasant to be able to speak without reserve or evasion, pleasant to be known surely for what you are (with exceptions, of course), pleasant to feel that there cannot be any sudden occasion to be a cat or a flea.

Elya enjoyed her morning among the secretarial staff of the Chinese Embassy. There was no need to be Miss Gabriel there. They knew her for who she was, which was to their advantage, as well as hers, for they made very full and confident use of her knowledge of a language which was native to them, and yet, to her, so much more completely known.

The ambassador himself consulted her upon the wording of a dispatch which he was about to send to Peking, and which he wished to make most delicately offensive, in such a way that it could not be resented without admission that he had been badly instructed, and his better judgement overruled, to his country's loss.

He was not entirely dissatisfied with the ironic flatteries which he had composed, but when Elya had concentrated upon it all the subtlety of language in her control, he knew it to be a masterpiece that the president would writhe as he read. But he would not dare to recall one who had such command of elusive words that he might be potent to shake his seat.

To Elya, the composing of that letter was the most impish joy she had known since she had turned her eyes to the Solar System, thinking to make her exile a pleasant interlude to censured celestial pranks.

Desire to experience the sharp contrast to that civilised urbanity led her to go straight on to the Russian Embassy, which, for that afternoon, she had been under no definite engagement to do. There was no question there of her being entitled to the welcome appropriate to those who come from supernal spheres. Within the Russian Embassy, common sense ruled—and human nature was understood. Evil motives must be assumed until disproved by exhaustive tests. That should be evident to a child of ten. An intelligent man does not expect truth. He awaits lies.

Judged by these standards, Elya was a liar of audacity unequalled in their ample experience. But, while sure of that, they yet felt that she was of a quality difficult to assess. A liar should come in a plausible garb of truth, which she had not done.

Her knowledge of Russian was faultless, comprehensive, exceptional both in quality and kind. She could talk at their own level, and with a vocabulary far larger than it was customary for them to use. She could talk the slang of a Moscow slum with equal ease, and with equal range. That she had never been in Russia was a most evident lie. That was just where the trouble lay. It was so blatant a lie that to tell it was waste of words. Then what could the game be?

What subtle wile of the British Foreign Office had sent the woman to them? Asking them mendaciously for an opinion upon that which they doubtless already knew? At the simplest explanation she was a spy, who was to win their confidence and betray it to her employers. And yet, if that were so, how crudely it was being done. Was it hoped that she would gain a lover, who would betray his country to win her? Her loveliness made it seem the most probable explanation. And it was a contingency which the ambassador must watch with a wary mind. For he was separated from his wife, and he suspected that his chauffeur had special instructions to report any feminine entanglements through which his integrity might be assailed, in addition to the normal reports concerning his conduct which he knew that the Third Secretary dispatched every week to Moscow. Was it not even possible that it was the Kremlin which had sent her to test his power of resistance and to safe-conduct his indiscretions, if such there should be?

If that were true, he knew that an adverse report from her, whether true or false, would be utter ruin for him. He would be summoned back to Moscow with the knowledge that he would be almost certainly liquidated; and the alternative would be to lose his Russian estates, and remain a penniless exile on foreign soil. To treat her too intimately or too distantly might equally be dangerous—and, of course, that might not be the explanation at all.

"Excellency," the Third Secretary said, "Miss Gabriel is here again. She says that it is you she wishes to see."

"Dromski," he replied, "it is a wish which I do not share."

"Shall I send her away?"

"You had better question her in your own way. She is a clear fraud, and it may be important that we should know her for what she is."

"With deference, Excellency, is it not a mystery which yourself, rather than those beneath you, should be equal to probe?"

Mr. Vilinski looked in a moment of pregnant silence at a subordinate whose neck it would have been a pleasure to wring. Then he said: "You may be right. There is certainly something queer about her which we should be active to understand. But it is a matter on which two opinions may be better than one. You shall bring her in, and stay with me, that she may be assessed by your shrewdness, which is often greater than mine."

While this conversation proceeded, Miss Gabriel sat alone with Alexis Slimski, the junior clerk of the embassy, a hard-featured, black-eyed young man whose aspect she did not approve.

He was a self-confident youth of aggressive temperament and a bold ambition. He looked to use the opportunities of the position he held for his own rapid advancement, with few scruples as to the methods he might employ. He already had the important assignment of spying on the Third Secretary and the ambassador's chauffeur, so that Moscow could be assured that they did not fail in their duty of spying upon the ambassador; and he was in the singular position, or so he thought (it must end somewhere!), of being free from supervision himself, and surely it would be imbecility to fail to turn such an opportunity to his own advantage.

He observed the radiant loveliness of the ambiguous visitor whom Sir Andrew Weyleigh had thrust upon them with more attention than she was likely to give to him. Was there not enigma here which it could be to his advantage to solve? Nothing which could be twisted into sinister accusations against the watchers or him they watched?

He asked, in what he supposed to be an ingratiating manner: "I expect you find this climate very pleasant, after what you'd been used to before?"

Elya countered, with brief simplicity: "Why?"

It was a less informative response than he had hoped to obtain, but he gambled boldly for the assent which he might luckily gain, or the denial which could be met by a further query: "Because I know how hot Moscow is at this time of year."

"But I don't. The place I came from's millions of miles away, and, unless we want it changed, the heat's always the same."

"You mean you've got central heating?"

"You wouldn't understand. It's millions of miles away, and not like it is here."

Mr. Slimski grinned affably. He said: "You know, you can't kid me like that. You don't come millions of miles in a week. If you'd come that far you'd be a bit older than you are now."

Elya was naturally puzzled by this reply. Even her agile mind could not readily descend to the depth of stupidity which it exposed. She said patiently: "But there is no sense in that. Distance is not absolute in relation to time."

"I don't even know what you think I mean. Distance is just what it is. A million miles is ten times a hundred thousand. Juggling with words couldn't alter that."

"I think I do know what you think you mean, and it's about the most absolute bosh..."—actually she used a Moscow slang word for which there is no exact English equivalent—"...that could come out of a human mouth."

"You're not very polite, Miss Gabriel. But it's plain sense to me."

"I'm never polite to anyone, because I don't like being rude. But I wonder how you'll find an answer to this: suppose you walk across the room. It's not far, and won't take you long. And suppose you have—well, say a cheesemite— You know what that is, don't you?"

"Yes. I know that."

"Well, I'm never quite sure. I can't assume anyone knows anything without getting upset now and then. Suppose you had a cheesemite in your pocket. Would it cross the room at the same rate as yourself?"

"I suppose there's a catch in that. It might be crawling the other way."

"There was no catch at all. I meant if it were in the same place in your pocket the whole time."

"Then the answer's yes."

"But it would have taken it hundreds of times longer on its own legs."

"I expect it might. But there's no puzzle in that. It's because it's smaller than I. It would be as though I got into a train."

"So it would," she answered, in her usual friendly equable manner. "But you can't use brains that you haven't got. It's not fair to expect. Still, you might try thinking it out."

What he would have answered to this must remain unknown, for it was at this point that Mr. Dromski returned to invite her into the ambassador's room.

Mr. Slimski was left to think: "She talks the most absolute rot that I ever heard. But acting the fool may be no less than a clever trick. She certainly played me along so that I learnt nothing from her"—while Elya, entirely unaware of having done anything more than meet human stupidity with patient placid replies, went on to an encounter with sharper wits, though they might be less sure of themselves.

CHAPTER FOURTEEN

EMBASSIES DIFFER

It was no more than two minutes that Mr. Vilinski was alone, while his secretary was bringing Miss Gabriel in, but it is possible to conceive an audacious idea in less time than that—and how audacious his conception was could not be adequately realised by one who did not perceive the truth with the simpler, sounder logic of the Chinese.

"We are grateful to you, Miss Gabriel," he said affably, "that you have been so prompt in paying us a second visit," and as he said it he pushed a slip of paper toward Mr. Dromski, on which he had scribbled: *Bait for Surrell?*

The secretary read it; looked puzzled, then surprised, and then changed his expression to the acquiescent approval which he was expected to show.

The ambassador went on: "There is a matter on which you may be able to give us important help, for which we shall be willing to pay on a most liberal scale."

"Would you give me two hundred pounds?"

Mr. Vilinski hesitated at this evidence that others could be audacious, as well as he. But he knew that, should the enterprise be successful, it would be held to justify even a larger payment than that. He said: "I would give you twenty now, and eighty on it being done."

"Would it be easy to do?"

"I should think it would be quite easy for you."

"Would it take long?"

"It might be done in a few hours. Say, two days at the most."

"When can you give me the twenty pounds?"

"I should like to have your undertaking first that you will carry it through."

"If it's easy, and won't take long, I can promise that. I told Leonard that I could get money quickly."

The ambassador saw an unexpected opportunity of gaining some information concerning her background or antecedents. He asked: "Leonard being a friend?"

"Only a man I was staying with. We needn't talk about him."

He did not pursue the subject, but his opinion of her suitability for the purpose he had in view rose many degrees. Evidently the man with whom she had been living had not been able to satisfy her financial demands, and she had told him that she could do better for herself by discarding him, which she was proceeding to prove. Perhaps it would be best to give her the money at once, as for a bargain already made. He rose, opened a small safe in the wall behind his chair, and she gave him smiling thanks as the notes disappeared in her bag.

"Now," he said, "I will explain to you what I want you to do. There is a man living at 38a Dover street named Rodney Surrell—Dromski, you've got a photograph of him, haven't you? Well, get it, and let Miss Gabriel see it.

I don't want her to take it away, but just to have a good look. We mustn't risk her hooking on the wrong man. Well, he usually goes to the Pickthall Grill in Piccadilly for lunch. He goes at one-thirty, when they're full up, but they reserve him a seat in the corner that's to the right of anyone going in. I want you to get seated as close to his place as you can—that means getting there a good deal earlier, to make sure—and make friends with him there. Of course, you won't let him know that you've ever heard of him before. I've only given you his name and address so that you can make sure that you've got the right man. I want you to ask him to go home with you to this address…"—he handed her a small printed card—"…which you will tell him is yours. You'll get a taxi, and you'll find the maid there will know your name, and will let you in."

"Yes," Elya agreed readily. "I could do that. I expect he'll come to my table like Leonard did."

"I expect he will, if you look at him in the right way, and you'll know how to do that."

"I didn't have to look at Leonard at all."

"Well, if you don't find it necessary, that will be all the better. He's a very nervous, suspicious man, and you've got to let him feel that it's he that's running after you."

"Oh, I could do that! That's just how it would be. But suppose he's the sort of man I shouldn't like to be with?"

"That's how you'll be earning the hundred pounds."

"Yes," she replied, "so I should." But it was still in a doubtful voice, causing the ambassador to wonder whether she were thinking out for a higher fee. But it was at this moment that Mr. Dromski returned, and when the photograph was in her hands her expression changed.

"I like him better than Leonard," she said happily, as though to herself. "I think he's got a nicer face, and a much better figure. But," she turned her eyes to the secretary to ask, "but you can't tell everything while they've got their clothes on, can you?"

Mr. Dromski replied that he should think you could make a good guess, to which she rejoined that she expected she would when she had had more experience, and might have continued to develop the conversation on these lines had not Mr. Vilinski, whose mind was fluctuating between a conviction that she was almost miraculously suitable for the part she was asked to play, and fear that she would spoil everything by almost incredible gaucherie, interposed to say: "Miss Gabriel, I want you to understand that we shall be paying you to do exactly as I have asked, neither more nor less. If you contrive so that Mr. Surrell accompanies you to the house, you will have eighty pounds tomorrow. I don't ask you to do anything more than that. But nothing less will be any good, and I'm trusting you to play your cards in the right way."

"I haven't tried playing cards yet, but I know what you mean. I'll get him there if he's as silly as most men are. But what am I to do after that?"

"You won't have to worry about anything further. When you've got him there it will be the end of the matter, as far as you are concerned."

"I don't think that's sense. And I think an ambassador must be a sensible man. Something *must* happen. He'll either stay or he'll go away. I think there's something you don't want me to know."

The words might have the sound of a challenge, but she looked at him with such sweet simplicity that his diplomatic instinct, which rarely failed, prompted the most effective reply.

"Miss Gabriel," he said, with a smile which was only second to hers, "if you think there's something I don't want you to know, don't you think it might be courteous not to enquire? If I give you my word that we ask you to do nothing more than to take Mr. Surrell to the address you have, isn't it all that you need to know? After that, you can do, or not do, anything that you like. You'll have the eighty pounds from us just the same.

"But if you want to get the money, you'll do well to keep in mind that he's a nervous man, and if you let him think that you're running after him, or that you ever heard of him before, you won't get him to move a yard. I tell you this because I can see that you want to earn the money, and you can't if you don't keep it in mind."

"Oh, that's all right," she replied confidently. "I never forget anything. Will it be a long ride to the house?"

"About four miles. You must make it seem as short to him as you can."

"You mean kiss him and things like that?" She asked, with some distaste in her voice. Then she looked at the photograph again, and her serenity was resumed. "I dare say," she said, "it won't seem very long."

"No," he agreed, with equal confidence. "I don't think it will."

CHAPTER FIFTEEN

THE SEDUCTION OF MR. SURRELL

Mr. Surrell entered the restaurant at one twenty-seven, and zigzagged a way to his usual corner without looking right or left. He took his seat without observing the radiant beauty of the girl at the next table, who, having already drawn her meal out to a length of forty-five minutes, was now conscious that the good work could not be continued forever, even by her, and toyed with that which, though the menu gave it a more recondite name, her perfect English would have described as strawberry ice.

She looked at a man who was unconscious of her, and thought: "He's better than the photograph. Better shoulders. And both sides of his face are alike, even his ears. I wonder what the taxi etiquette is exactly. Ought I to begin, or to wait for him? I'm almost certain I saw a girl tickling a man's neck this morning, when we pulled up at the lights. I can't see much point in that. Perhaps I shall when I've been a girl rather longer than I have now.

"I wonder whether he's got any brains. Probably not. I haven't met anyone yet who has. Unless it were Sir Andrew. (I suppose they'd say was for were. It's a great nuisance having to remember to say so many words wrong all the time. But most of them seem able to do it without any effort at all.) I certainly shouldn't call him a fool. And then, of course, there are the Chinese."

She turned her glance away from her main interest for a moment, a waiter intervening between them, and saw Mr. Slimski seated on the further side of the room, with his eyes on her. She thought: "I wonder whether Mr. Surrell knows him. If so, it's a silly thing to be here. But they *are* silly. I should be sillier still if I couldn't see that. And how silly they think I am!"

The last reflection was comment on the obtuseness (but it might have been lack of scruple) which they had imputed to her regarding the use to which she was being put. But she would have been enigma to wiser men than they were ever likely to be.

Now Mr. Surrell had given his order and the waiter had gone away. She took another spoonful of ice, and glanced casually in his direction. She was pleased to know that there was nothing casual in the way in which he was looking at her.

Elya might have exceptional standards of judgement, but most girls would have been pleased by that which her glance had met. Mr. Surrell was slim without being thin. He was young without being immature. He was dark without being swarthy. Handsome without being effeminate. His glance was confident without being rudely bold. He looked self-assured but without arrogance, quietly aware that he would be unlikely to encounter a difficulty with which he would be unequal to deal. The one thing that he did *not* resemble was the description that Mr. Vilinski had given—that of a nervous, cautious man.

Yet, she reflected, it was a matter on which it was improbable that the ambassador would have wished to mislead her. With an acumen which would have astonished the Russians' tortuous minds, she saw confirmation of the guess she had already made, and further light on that which she had been hired to do. Mr. Surrell was at ease in a populous place. She was to lure him to one of an opposite kind, and she would not find it an easy matter.

She saw a challenge in this at which her impish humour waked to a determination that victory should be hers. She remembered the eighty pounds, which she did not propose to lose. But might not she keep the bargain she had made with most literal truth, gain her reward, and yet avert the consequences which they designed? It was a problem to which her mind leapt with a dancing joy.

She glanced at him again. He was still looking at her. There was satisfaction in that. And then their eyes met in a curiously intimate way, and she became aware of a strange bewildering emotion that she had never known before either in heavenly or earthly spheres. She felt shy.

She had already been conscious of amorous tendencies, which she approved. They were delicious in themselves, and suggested all sorts of fun to her agile and lawless mind. But this was something of which she had neither previous experience or present desire—and which she could not control.

Her eyes fell, but her next action was prompted by the simple logic which ruled her mind. She remembered the sign of ownership which allocated women were expected to wear. It was to show him that she was eligible for pursuit by the human code that she laid an ungloved hand on the table, so that its integrity would be easy to see.

As her heartbeats slackened, she made a resolute effort, and looked at him again. Again their eyes met, and though there was no repetition of the first experience, she was aware of an instant smiling response at which a new sensation came which she had never experienced before in any life she had known. She felt young.

So she sat while he went through a four-course meal, lifting a cup of coffee at intervals to her lips, with care that it should not be entirely consumed, it being the shallow pretext for lingering as she did.

And that simple logical faculty which contrasted with the more complex mental processes which control the actions of men told her, as she sat silently there, that it was all *wrong*. She wasn't moving to his table, nor he to hers. They were making no progress at all. And now he was rising to go.

She would certainly have followed him out, to whatever end, though for the moment, in the stress of this strange emotion, she had forgotten the purpose for which she had come. But he did not go. He paused before her. He looked down on her with smiling admiring eyes. He said: "Forgive me asking, but you don't seem to have much to do, and I've got nothing at all. Suppose we go to a show together this afternoon, with no implication on either side? You could always tell me where to get off."

Her inclination to candour joined with her love of hazard to shape her instant reply: "I don't mind doing that, if you leave me to choose what the show shall be, which won't be anything you expect."

"That's soon agreed."

"If I ask you to do a dangerous thing, which will be worth eighty pounds to me, will you promise not to refuse?"

"I would not refuse anything which would be to your advantage, and which you should seriously ask me to do."

"Then I'd better tell you just what it is."

So she proceeded to do, concluding with: "I feel sure they mean to do something nasty to you, and you'll understand why, more likely than not. But, if you'll trust me, I think I can stop that."

He sat down now, on the other side of the little table. He said: "Perhaps you wouldn't mind telling me how?"

"I would if I thought you'd believe, but…. Oh, Slimski's going. He's one of them who's been watching us from the other side of the room. I expect he thinks I've hooked you now that he's seen us talking together, and he's gone to tell them what to expect."

"No doubt he has. Can you tell me what sort he is?"

"He's just small and dark and coarse, with a mean, bullying look. If he were among a score, and you should pick out the worst, it would be he, unless another of them were there."

"It is a particularly clear description. I just want to telephone for a moment, and when I come back I shall have something interesting to tell you."

"Very well, then; I'll wait."

He went out to the hall, where there are two telephone booths side by side, but when he saw that one of them was occupied by the gentleman who had been so clearly described, he drew back unobserved, until he was assured that Slimski had left. Then he had a short conversation which seemed to be of a satisfactory nature, if it could be judged by the smile of satisfaction with which he returned to the dining room.

"I will come with you," he said, as he sat down at Elya's table again, "as I have promised to do. But I must tell you exactly the risk I run, and perhaps (apart from anything I may contrive for my own defence) you will then tell me what is in your own mind, which would save my life, and still enable you to claim the reward, as you are so clearly anxious to do."

"Yes, I am. I owe Laura sixty pounds. And there are a lot more clothes that I want to buy."

"You make everything clear. Now I will tell you why they have offered you so large a bribe for that which they foresaw might not be easy to do. I was in Moscow two years ago, where I was the representative of one of the largest engineering firms in this country. I don't suppose the name would mean anything to you, but when it went into liquidation it was what the newspapers call a sensational event."

"I know that funny word. I know all about journalese. I wish you could tell me about liquidation. But I suppose you'd better go on with your own tale."

"Yes, I think I had. I had trusted them. I had had good reasons for that. When they failed, not only did they owe me a large sum, but I had entered into personal obligations in Moscow on their behalf. Worse than that, I had persuaded the Russian Government to pay them a large sum on account of machinery they were manufacturing for it, which was supposed to be ready for despatch, but which they were never likely to see. When I heard what was happening, I decided to return to England at once, but I was refused permission to leave the country.

"After being kept in suspense for many weeks, waiting for a visa I did not get, I was invited to see the Prefect of Police, and offered cancellation of the obligations I had incurred if I would obtain secret information which it was suggested to me that I could do without treachery to my own country. I asked time to consider the proposition, and got in touch with the British Embassy there, after which I acted on their advice. I let them think me a hired traitor for some time, and that went on till I was back here, but they got suspicious, and I had a warning not to risk putting myself in their hands again. They've summoned me now several times, and I haven't gone, so if they were suspicious before, you can guess what they are now."

"Yes. It's about what I expected to hear. When I first heard about men on Earth, and how they ate and slept and kept their skins clean every day for fifty years, or perhaps twice that, I thought how dreadfully bored they must get, and how glad when they could die. I didn't see that they might be playing games all the time."

"You mean that you didn't see that you might go on playing games when you'd grown up? Well, that's putting it cheerfully. What do you think they're planning to do to me?"

"I should think they'll kill you, if they can, more likely than not. And when they've failed, I hope that you will owe something to me."

"It's pleasant to hear that it's your programme that they shall fail. Actually, they might do worse than kill me, if they should get me alone. I might be third-degreed, if you understand that."

"Yes, I do. But what they don't understand is that I could do worse to them."

"Do you mind telling me how?"

Elya was silent for a moment. She would like him to feel that she might not be impotent at a crisis, but how could that be, if she should tell less than the truth? And would the truth obstruct the happy intimacy which was now established between them? She wished she had said less, but saw that she had gone too far on a doubtful road, and must continue now. She said: "Well, I know you'll find it hard to believe, but I am an angel. I'm not really a girl. At least, I am a girl now; but I was an angel before."

"I don't wonder that people should call you that."

"You think I'm joking. But if you like to telephone Sir Andrew Weyleigh…. He's at Godalming, at—"

"No. He returned to Whitehall this morning. It was to him that I have just been speaking."

"Well, it doesn't matter where he is, if you know. He's seen me go out of the room like a cat, and come back as I am now, and get into my clothes. He'll tell you I do unexpected things, and that you'll be safe with me. You don't believe me," she went on in a changed voice, bitter with regret. "I wish I hadn't told you what I can do," and as she spoke her eyes filled with the first tears she had ever shed.

"Please don't say that," he answered, in a distress which, even in her own discomfiture, it was pleasant to see. "I may not understand, but that doesn't mean that I don't believe. All the same, I doubt whether it would be safe to rely on conjuring tricks with them, however cleverly they might be done."

"But they're not conjuring tricks," she said desperately. "I don't know what you'll think, but you've got to know now. You'd better telephone Sir Andrew again."

"So I will if you wish. But he won't tell me anything that'll make me think less of you than I do now."

"Perhaps not. But he'll make you think differently. That's what I'm afraid of."

"Then I won't telephone him, and you'll have nothing to fear."

She gave way easily, leaving a perilous path, and reverted to a trouble which lay restlessly at the back of her mind. "I don't know that I've done right in telling you all I have. I shouldn't have done it if you hadn't promised to come. And then it seemed the right thing to do."

"It is a rather complicated question of ethics, and I think you might have done a good deal worse than you have. Anyway, I'm not the one to complain. But don't you think it's about time for us to go?"

Two minutes later, Mr. Slimski, who had not retired further than to the other side of the road, and had become anxiously doubtful of what could delay their appearance for so long a time, had the satisfaction of telephoning that he had seen them get into a taxi together, and that the seduction of Mr. Surrell had been achieved.

CHAPTER SIXTEEN

THE ADVENTURE OF FISHPOND HOUSE

Elya looked at the man beside her, whose arm, as she supposed, should have been drawing her toward him, but who showed no such immediate intention, though she was correctly sure that the slightest encouragement would result in all that her imagination would have forecast; and she had a third emotional experience that was without precedent in her uninhibited existence—diffidence of herself, and of what she projected to do. And, surprisingly, she was aware that the man beside her, whom she had judged to be confident and assertive in speech and act, had the same impulse, and the same diffidence as herself.

But she could not easily be silent upon any theme that engaged her mind. She said: "I don't wonder they look so sullen."

"I don't suppose I should either, if I knew who they are."

"The taxi drivers, of course, because they never get in at the back."

He considered this. "You mean they'd have better company if they did?"

"Yes. And something better than driving to do."

"Such as—?" he smiled, and his arm was around her now.

It was three minutes later that she said: "Now I know I did the right thing when I decided to be a girl."

"You mean you've never been kissed before?"

"Nor behind," she answered, with angelic levity which was natural to her when excited to any pleasant emotion, and found it to be a remark for which the back of her neck must pay.

But however much pleasure she might find in the game which she was beginning to play, she was always of a practical mind, and it was she who said, a moment later: "Don't you think we'd better stop being silly, and decide what we're to do, so that we don't have anything going wrong? We shall have the first minutes for sure, because they won't try to do anything much to you while I'm there, because they won't want me to know; and that ought to be long enough for us to put them how we want them to be."

"It is a shrewd idea. But I must suggest that there is one possibility which it overlooks. They may not attach any importance to your being alive tomorrow, even to collect what you will have earned."

"You mean they may be planning to kill me too?"

"You might otherwise be a dangerous witness."

"Well," she said, with a light amusement which he had not expected to rouse," they'll get a surprise if they try that."

"You mean it would be a more formidable proposition than dealing with me?"

"It would be *different*. They'd have to be as quick as a cat's jump, and they might find they'd been too slow, even then. The only trouble is getting back into my clothes, and I've thought and thought, and I can't see any way to overcome that."

"Couldn't you make it a little clearer?"

"I could if it would be any use. The trouble is that I have to do it to make people believe. I can turn myself into any creature I like, and back again in less time than it takes for a bullet to leave a gun. But the trouble is that I have to leave my clothes on the floor. You can see what a mess it would be if I tried it now."

"You really ask me to believe that?"

"Well, it's the truth, and you can't have a better reason. But no one will believe me unless they've seen, and that's why I wanted you to phone Sir Andrew."

"You tell me seriously that you can transform yourself into other creatures?"

"Yes, angels—I mean my kind of angels—can."

"Well, we won't discuss that, if you'll promise that you'll never try to do it again."

"I won't unless there's a very great need."

"I want an absolute promise, please. I don't want to feel I'm like the man in the fable who found that the woman he'd married could be a cat in the night."

"*Married?* You really mean—? Well, we might. After all, I don't see why not, for a time at least. But about that cat, I shouldn't think it was a fable at all. It was just something people wouldn't believe, as you won't now. But if we go on like this we shall be at Fishpond House before we've decided who's to deal the first card, and what it's to be. Have you got any guns?"

"I've got one."

"The kind that keeps going off? Then that ought to do. When we get out, I'll go first to the door, as it's natural that I should. You can come a few steps behind, and give me time to look round. You needn't trouble about me. I can take good care of myself. But if my clothes fall in a heap, you'll know there's trouble about two feet ahead, and you'll shoot quickly, and shoot to kill. If I keep as I am now, you'll come on with your gun ready, and listen to what I say."

"You feel sure that the orders should come from you?"

"I don't want you to get hurt. And I know the kind of devils they are. (Not that they are devils really. I'll tell you about that when we've got more time.) But there may not be any row at the door, as they say that a girl will open it when I ring. Not that we can tell much from that. I suppose you know what girls are. They're not all angels like me. There's a car following us. It's been doing that since we turned off the Edgware Road, and probably before that."

"You don't miss much. Yes, I arranged that when I phoned. It's been on our trail since we left the restaurant. It may look like a worn-out Ford, privately owned. But it has an engine which might outpace anything on the road, and the elderly gentleman seated beside the chauffeur has a sub-machinegun across his knees."

"I don't see that they'll be any use, unless you're mean enough to give me away, and I can't think that. We've got to go up to the door alone."

"So we shall. The Ford will drive on, and turn round, and pull up on the other side of the road. You see I've looked further ahead than you, and I'm hoping to pick up one or two whom we can lock up for the night."

"Then it looks as though they'll have to wait a good distance away."

"Yes. I see that now."

So it was. For Fishpond House stood far back from the road in its own grounds, and as they spoke they stopped before iron gates which the driver must descend to open. They saw a wide lawn, and a low red brick façade, with a background of beech and oak, through which shone a gleam of water from the pond which gave its name to the house.

A maid servant opened the door, and held it back with routine indifference for them to enter, as though their own home. A door stood wide on the right hand side of the softly-carpeted hall, through which Elya led confidently, resolved to be the first to explore whatever they were to meet. But she came to no more than an empty lounge, suggestive of quiet comfort and ease.

Her companion followed her, and the maid, with a demurely deferential manner, closed the door behind him as she withdrew.

Elya looked round the empty room. She looked out of the window, and said: "The taxi's still at the door."

"Well, I understood that you were not expected to stay."

"But how should he know that?"

Before he could reply, the maid re-entered the room. "Could I have a word with you, madam?" She asked respectfully, as she drew back into the hall.

Elya followed her at once.

The girl said: "We knew you wished to go back, madam, so Parkins told the taxi to wait."

Elya merely said: "Thank you."

A moment later Rodney Surrell, looking out of the lounge window, saw her enter the taxi, and drive away.

"So that's that," he thought, with a natural bitterness, seeing himself as the fool of the piece, and one who could not avoid a snare even when he had been cynically told what it was intended to be.

He turned from the window as the door opened again, and saw that Mr. Dromski had entered. The Third Secretary advanced to the table, drew out a chair, and sat down. He said: "Shall we have a quiet talk? I will tell you at once that I am unarmed, and you can shoot me if you think that it will be any advantage to do so. But you would be consigning yourself to a death of particularly unpleasant details, which you may avoid if you will."

He waved his hand toward a chair on the opposite side of the table, but it was a gesture to which Mr. Surrell did not respond. He said: "Can you tell me why I should wish to shoot you? We have no quarrel so far as I am aware."

"It is not I, it is Russia that you have failed."

"Russia is strong enough to get along without me," Mr. Surrell replied lightly, though he saw that Elya's desertion might have left him in greater peril than he had expected to meet. But what dementia could have led him to expect support from a sinewless chattering girl, even if she had not been in Russian pay? And yet his mind, analytical even at such a moment as that, admitted to himself that it had been very cleverly done. Nothing but the audacity of telling him that she had been hired for his undoing might have succeeded in drawing him to this deadly trap. "But if I have failed her, that is no reason for shooting you."

"None at all. But it is a reason why you must die."

"To which I am supposed to assent?"

"You will find that you have no choice. But the details are for you to decide. If you will answer a few questions with the frankness which the occasion requires, you will have nothing to fear beyond being knocked on the head with the efficiency which may be expected from one who is practised in what he does, and thrown into the pond, where you will be most useful to feed the eels. But if you should be stubborn, you would be dealt with in a quite different way. You are doubtless familiar with a form of execution which has been more or less popular in Russia for many centuries past—that of being impaled? Yes, I can see that you are. The lake is about five feet deep, and under water there is a suitable stake on which you would be firmly fixed, but so that your feet would not touch the lake bottom. It is the peculiar feature of this unhurried form of execution that, though the injuries you would receive would be such that it would be of no lasting benefit to you should you be taken off the stake in the next minute, yet the upward penetration would be so gradual that you might live for two or three days, or somewhat longer under favourable circumstances; but it is only fair to tell you that the period would be shortened to an extent on which your guess is as good as mine by the fact that the eels are numerous, and that such portions of you as would be underwater (would two-thirds be an approximately accurate estimate?) would be most welcome to them. It is a prospect which does not disturb your mind?"

"No, I can't say that it does."

"Then I may reasonably assume that you do not intend to act in such a manner that this experience must be yours?"

Mr. Surrell, who was feeling in much better spirits than he had done a few minutes before, smiled slightly as he replied: "Yes, I think you may."

The fact was that his mind was largely occupied in controlling his inclination to look toward the door, which might turn Mr. Dromski's eyes in the same direction. For the last minute he had been obliquely aware that it was being pushed open in a manner so gradual and silent that it was reasonable to conclude that there was someone in the room for whom surprise was designed, which was unlikely to be himself.

Now he knew, though without a direct glance, that a very large dog had come into the room, and was advancing over the carpet with soundless feet, behind the secretary's chair.

The moment came when he could look with the same sardonic glance at Mr. Dromski and the dog, which was directly behind him.

He felt sure that it was not the secretary's dog, and its fierce eyes and stealthy movements were not suggestive of friendly purpose in what it did. But, in fact, it did him no vital harm.

Strong teeth closed on a chair leg, which was pulled suddenly back. With not time even for a cry of alarm, Mr. Dromski's hindquarters bumped heavily on the floor, where he lay in an awkward sprawl.

Next moment, a dog's foot was holding him down, with a pressure which made breathing hard. He saw an open mouth, with white teeth gleaming a few inches above his throat.

"Call the brute off," he screamed. "If anything happens to me you'll be lucky if they only skin you alive."

"The dog," Mr. Surrell replied pleasantly, "is not mine, and I have no reason to suppose that he would listen to me."

"Then shoot him, can't you, and I'll give you a better break than you could have hoped to have a moment ago."

But Mr. Surrell had become doubtful of the accuracy of his assertion that the dog would not listen to him. She had raised her head, and was looking round as though asking what she should do next. There was an atmosphere of understanding between them, more difficult to comprehend than accept.

He crossed the room to the prostrate man, and with no fear of the proximity of the gaping jaws, searched his pockets, and withdrew the gun which he had said that he had not got.

He said: "Let him get up now, if you like," as though speaking to a human colleague, and the dog moved backward. Mr. Dromski rose, a breathless and frightened man.

Mr. Surrell looked at the dog, and she looked at him, and it would be difficult to say which was the more puzzled as to what the next move should be.

When Elya had driven away in accordance with the suggestion the maid servant had made, it had not been with any intention of abandoning her companion to whatever fate might be intended for him. It was not flight, but a strategic move to the rear.

Let them think that she had conformed to the plan which had been dictated to her, and she would be able to return unsuspected for such interference as she would be most competent to contrive. (And, incidentally, would she not have made sure of the eighty pounds which she was resolved that she would not lose?) As the taxi had borne her away, she was confronted by the difficulty which vexed her before, and it was now in a worse form. "What," she asked herself, using an emphatic adjective which her comprehensive knowledge of English did not omit "what about these damnable clothes?"

Well, they must just take their chance, for there was nothing else to be done.

She saw that it would be folly to return in her own womanly form, and she was not willing to delay being on the scene of a certain crisis the nature of which she could not foresee.

The driver did not observe that a swallow shot from the open window of the moving vehicle, and when he looked round a moment later for instructions as to where she wished him to go, he saw only a heap of clothes on the seat, and sagging on to the floor.

Meanwhile Elya had flown into an open window on the first floor of Fishpond House, and perched for one reconnoitring moment on the foot-rail of a bed in an empty room. She saw that the door was not latched, but so nearly shut that she could not fly through it. Neither could she open it in her adopted form. It was a case for a large dog.

Next moment she had pulled open the door in the incarnation which was so clearly required.

She went along a vacant landing, and silently down the stairs. She heard voices from both sides of the hall. There was a man on guard in the hall who stood with his back to her, and there was a gun in his hand. With one great leap she bore him down, and her teeth closed in the back of his neck with a fatal crunch. She repented next moment, though the necessity had appeared extreme. But if you are a dog, can a dog's impulses be always controlled?

Being satisfied that he was dead, she wiped her jaws on his clothes, and proceeded to listen from door to door till she heard the voice of the man she sought through one which had not been shut.

So she had come to where she now was, and the dilemma in which she stood. Should she continue to be a dog? Could she be a girl again without those—yes, those *damnable* clothes, which must be forever gone?

Even had she had the use of a human voice, she was unsure what it would be best to propose. What to do with the frightened Dromski, whose vicious eyes flickered toward the door through which he hoped that rescue would come, ignorant that the one who should have been alert lay dead in the hall? How they could overcome their opponents, or escape unseen? Now that the man who lay dead had the deep incisions of a dog's teeth in his neck, so that it had become a particularly dangerous animal for her to continue to be?

Yet in what other guise could she now remain beside him, and any common purpose be understood between them?

It was evident that, unless they would engage all the men in the house (about twenty at her best guess) in desperate combat, they must find some road of escape, or seek precarious delay until rescue might come through the friends they had left in the road.

She thought (which was not entirely true) that she understood the position better than he, and her final decision was that she would assume control of their movements, and trust to his following hers when he should see that it would be the only course by which they would remain together.

Between house and road there was a lawn far too wide to give reasonable hope that they could cross it without detection. They would become targets for more bullets than would be likely to go astray.

But behind the house was a wooded space. There were trees and water. Essential cover from bullets. Better prospect of evading pursuit.

The guard in the hall was dead, but others would not wait indefinitely for Dromski's return. They should seek escape without a moment's further delay.

That was clear. But how could they dispose of the man they held? To kill him was the obvious course, and she saw it to be one of which he could not logically complain.

But, except at a moment of extreme excitement, she found it to be something which the dog she was would be unwilling to do.

Also, it was a solution she was unable to propose, and on which agreement might not be easily reached. She knew that men, by a far-seeing provision of Nature, can be knocked on the head in such a way that they will be no more nuisance to anyone for a considerable period. But again, she could not propose it to her companion, and it might not be easy for her to do.

All these thoughts were instant as they stood in hesitation before their captive, and led to the conclusion that it was a preliminary matter with which she was unable to deal, and on which they could not consult, so that she must leave it to him.

And as she thought this, she became aware that he had come to the same decision, and that it was a matter to which he was not unequal.

While she guarded a man who was too frightened to move, she watched a heavy window-curtain being pulled down, within which Dromski was soon enveloped, without excessive regard for any difficulty in breathing which might result. When the bundle lay on the floor, tightly bound with curtain cords of satisfactory strength, with no more of its contents showing than the top of a head of coarse black hair, a gun butt was brought down upon it with stunning force, at which Dromski moaned and lay still.

But that did not conclude the operation. She had occasion to observe that her companion was a thorough man. Six similar blows were struck on other parts of the same skull. Avoiding the risk of fracture which must have resulted from a succession of blows on the same spot, he yet made sure that the unconsciousness at which he aimed would be of a thorough, and probably of an enduring quality.

Elya watched, and approved.

But she was resolved that there should be no dawdling in what they did. As the blows ceased to fall, she was already moving toward the door, which she drew open with a lifted paw. She looked cautiously out.

Everything was quiet and vacant. Without looking back to assure herself that she was followed, she went into the hall, and led the way toward the back of the house.

Mr. Surrell, with a gun in each hand, had no hesitation in deciding to follow. He did not identify the dog with Elya, which would have been unreasonable to expect, even after all she had said, but he had an instinctive conviction that it was all part of one sequent event, and his resentment against one who fled had unconsciously left his mind.

In the hall, he paused for a moment to look down on a dead man. There was no doubt of how he had died, and respect increased for an efficient and ruthless ally. He stooped down to collect a third weapon, which he dropped into his pocket, and went on down the passage, wishing that he could do so as silently as the one who led.

They left the house without opposition, or any sign that they had been observed, and gained the shelter of the trees. Having done that, it seemed obvious to him that they ought to skirt around the house, and regain the road, where they might expect that his friends would be waiting, if they had not already taken active measures for his relief.

But now Elya no longer led. She did not deviate, but she loitered at a time when speed seemed evidently preferable. Actually, she wanted to be behind, on which point she soon had her own way. Next moment, he was startled to hear Elya's voice, which said urgently: "Please don't look round. I'm here, but I've got nothing on. I mean no clothes. They're all in the taxi. But I must talk to you, and I can't while I'm a dog. I suppose you couldn't endure me without my clothes?"

"If you're serious, I certainly shouldn't mind, if you don't."

"Of course, I don't. Why should I...? If you really don't, you'd better turn round, and we can talk sensibly. I chose this place because there's a tree to sit on."

On this invitation, he turned round to see her seated in cool indifference to her nudity, on a fallen oak.

"You needn't stand," she went on. "There's room for two here. Where's the dog? Can't you understand even now? But you *must*. I was the dog. In about two minutes, I shall be one again. I know we mustn't stop here. But I've got to explain before there are other people about.

"I had to leave as I did, so that they should think I'd done what they wanted, and left you to them, and I couldn't come back as a girl, so I just changed into a bird, and then into a dog when I'd got back into the house. That was easy enough, but the trouble was I had to leave all my clothes, and *everything* in the taxi, so that I shall never see them again. I left my money. I left my bag. Of course, I've got some things in my rooms, but how am I to get back to them? I had to let you know, so that we can do sensible things. And I've got to make you believe. I haven't cared much about whether some people did, but I do about you. And that's partly why I'm going to change back into a dog while you're looking on."

"If you do that, I'll undertake to believe what I see, and, though it is outside most recorded human experience, I may add that I'm convinced now. But there is one point on which I may give you some reassurance. The things you left in the taxi will almost certainly be reported to the police, and can be recovered, though a credible explanation of what happened may not be easy to supply. And just one question—when you are a dog, can you understand what I say?"

"Yes, of course. I'm still an angel, though I've stopped being a girl. And, of course, I can't help being a dog too. But for that I don't suppose I should have killed that man as I did."

"Then I must be glad that you were, for it certainly needed doing. And now perhaps you'll change back to another—or will it be the same one as before?—because we really ought to be going on."

"Yes, I will. But you do like me as I am now?

As she asked this, her expression changed. She gave him a glance that was intimate and self-conscious. Her nudity became provocative and yet shy, but what might have followed cannot be known, for in the same instant he became conscious that she was not there. An impatient dog hurried ahead.

CHAPTER SEVENTEEN

THE HOUSE OF COMMONS

"As soon as you telephoned me," Sir Andrew said, "I rang up the Home Office, and they got in touch with Scotland Yard. The articles were at the Lost Property Office, and have now been sent back to Miss Gabriel. There was, of course, a reward to pay, but I have dealt with that, and it need not concern her. What I am interested to know is whether she claimed the money which had been promised to her by the Russian Embassy, which I strongly advised her not to attempt, as soon as I heard what had happened to you."

"So did I," Mr. Surrell replied, "but I wasted words. She said that she would be quite equal to them, and it was evidently money which she was determined to have. But in fact she had no difficulty at all. They paid it at once, without any suggestion that everything had not gone as they desired."

"They may have thought that she had done her part loyally to them, and had no responsibility for what followed. Anyway, it was the most diplomatic course to take.

If English character could be united with Russian brains…
but that is useless to hope."

"Well, I'm glad they paid her, whatever they thought;
and I'm glad she's got her other money back. The eighty
pounds went at once. She insisted on paying back a few
pounds I lent her to get some necessary clothes, although I
told her it didn't matter; and she's gone to repay sixty
pounds that she had from another woman. She says she
stole the clothes she was wearing, and talks of it as though
it were a good joke, but apart from that, I'd say she's as
transparently honest as any girl that I ever met."

"I am inclined to agree with you on that point. But, I
suppose she's been making you dance to her tune, and
proving to you that she is a flea?"

"Not exactly. She proved to me—if proof's the
word—that she can be a dog if she likes. But she certainly
saved my life. I owe her something for that. I wish I could
be sure what the truth is. I'd marry her if I thought I could.
But would it be like the old fable of the cat jumping out of
bed in the night?"

"If you're serious," Sir Andrew replied, with no levity
in his own voice, "I should say it would. But I'm not sure
that it would be dear at the price. And have you thought
how strongly it suggests that the old fable may not have
been a fable at all? There are so many tales—those of
werewolves, for instance—of the same kind. And doesn't
our own experience suggest that they were probably true,
but not believed by those who did not come into actual
contact with them? If you tell the next man you meet that
you've seen a girl turn into a dog, will he want to see it

himself, or just think that you're weak in the head, or making a silly joke?"

"Yes, it does make you think. But I'm forgetting what I promised to ask you. She wants to be introduced to members of the government—the Home Secretary in particular. And the Prime Minister. She says he can be sure of a huge majority at the next election, if he'll only listen to her. And that ought to make him jump."

"He'd jump for a lot less than that. He'd jump like—I won't say a flea. Like a kangaroo to get any majority at all. But how am I supposed to convince him that she could deliver the goods?"

"I think either of them would take your opinion seriously."

"But if I haven't got a serious opinion for them to take? The fact is that I'm inclined to believe she's really something—shall we say ultra-human? But I'm not sure, and I don't want to be one who's been befooled by some clever tricks."

"They're more than tricks. If you'd seen a man lying dead, with the back of his neck bitten through by a dog's teeth, and it had been done to get you out of a trap with which she needn't have interfered—"

"Yes," Sir Andrew replied. "I see how you feel, and I'm inclined to put my weight in the same scale. But I won't introduce her to Langford. It's too risky. He'd set the police on her, if she rubbed him the wrong way, more likely than not. But I'll tell the P.M. about her, and say I can't be sure whether she's genuine or a fake, and I want his opinion. He won't miss seeing her, if his curiosity's roused. You remember how he—"

"Yes. I see what you mean. I should say you couldn't do it a better way."

This conversation took place in Sir Andrew's White-hall office, and bore its fruit three days later, when Elya sat on the terrace of the House of Commons, eating straw-berries and cream with Rodney and Mr. Nixon—Nixon, the member she had acquired with her flat, and was ob-served by a gentlemen who strolled past her two or three times before taking the cigar from his mouth, pausing be-side her chair, and saying genially: "Will you please intro-duce me, Nixon?" To which Elya replied: "Oh, there's no need for that. I know you're the Prime Minister. Rodney, there's no need to get up. We can make room, if Sir Eden will bring a chair from the next table," which Sir Eden Mountford obediently proceeded to do.

A prime minister must be familiar with many varieties of bad manners from those he meets in a passing way. Some will be obsequious. Some bumptious. Some nerv-ous. Some persistent on points of unwelcome political or personal curiosities. But this friendly casual attitude was so noticeably unusual that he thought acutely: "I shouldn't wonder if Andrew really has got something here."

It was an opinion which did not lessen when Elya said pleasantly, as he sat down beside her: "I suppose you're still making more laws as hard as you can?"

"We have an exceptionally busy session."

"I expect you like being prime minister?"

"It is an honour—a mark of confidence—which I do not contemn."

Elya looked at him with laughing eyes. She said: "It sounded just like an answer. I suppose if I should ask a hundred questions you'd be able to go on in the same way. You must have to use a lot of words. Most people I talk to don't use many. Besides telling lies all the time. I think yours is a better way."

"It is a most generous interpretation."

"I never say unkind things, but I can't help telling the truth."

"It is an unusual qualification."

"Yes. I see that. I suppose I could tell lies, but is it worthwhile to try?"

"I should say that that is a proposition which could not be answered without important reservations. But you do not appear to be gravely incommoded by the disability. Or perhaps the disinclination would be a more accurate word. If that be so, would not any change be a hazard you need not take?"

"Well, I shan't try. It would be too much trouble for me."

"But is that what it would be? Most people find their trouble in a precisely opposite direction. I think, Miss Gabriel, that you may be inclined to depreciate—or should we say ignore?—your own excellence. To tell the exact truth must always be a most difficult art. The poet who wrote about simple truth and utmost skill may have expressed himself with inaccuracy—we will not say with untruth—obscurity may be a better word—or he may be commonly misunderstood."

"Suppose we stop wasting time, and have a real talk?"

"So we will. I am told that you have an infallible plan for winning the next election?"

"Yes. That's easy. You'd have to promise not to make any more laws."

"You think that would have a decisive consequence?"

"I don't think people *could* be silly enough not to support that. But if you wished to make extra sure, you could promise to repeal a few thousand of those there are."

"You think a few thousand would be enough?"

"Perhaps few was the wrong word. But that's how you'd have to begin. You might say you'd go on till there weren't more than people could learn say in five years, or perhaps ten. When they'd all been that long at what were left, they wouldn't refuse to let you slaughter a few more."

"It is a most fascinating idea. But have you thought of what the consequences would be when the laws were gone?"

"Yes, of course. Everyone would live a much happier life—except the lawyers, and even they might be happier when they'd found something better to do."

"Can you give me an example of a law that should be repealed?"

"I don't know very much about laws, except what a lot there are, and that you're expected to be making more, as fast as you can. But why not squash the one that stops people working?"

"I'm not sure that I know which one you mean."

"I don't suppose you are. That just shows what a mess you're in! I've been told that there's only one of that sort, because it doesn't matter what time other people work, or when they leave off. But people who keep shops can make a lot of trouble by shutting them up, and so you make them do it, whether they want to or not."

"It is a lucid statement of an illogical position which I am not concerned to defend. But may I conclude that this custom has been inconvenient to you?"

"You know custom isn't the right word. But it certainly has. Suppose you had to turn into a dog because all your clothes had gone off in a taxi, and you couldn't get any more in the evening, so that you could go back to your flat in your proper shape—or, anyway, in the shape that you had to have. You can't say that you'd like that."

"It is an experience that I have missed in an otherwise varied life. But I can appreciate how you felt. Would it be opportune to enquire how you got over the difficulty?

"I don't mind telling, if you mean that. Rodney here knows all about it, and I told Mr. Nixon—Nixon a few minutes ago. I had to go on being a dog while Rodney took me back in a taxi to my own flat. (And if any girl in a taxi should be a dog, she'd find out it would make a lot of difference in how she'd have to behave. But I needn't go into that now.) When we got to my flat—I mean outside— I had to stop being a dog, so that I could talk. I hadn't got a key, and we couldn't get in. I wanted Rodney to go down and take the one the porter has in the hall, and he didn't want to do that; and he didn't want me to go because I hadn't got any clothes—you know the fuss there always is about that—and while we were quarrelling the cleaning woman came along, and I changed back into a dog, but I was just a second too late, and she fainted at what she saw, which was the best thing she could do, because when she knew what was happening next, the keys were back on her belt, and we were both in the room, and the door locked, so that we could do what we liked. And Rodney felt a lot better about it when I'd got a dressing gown on, and he was very good about it, and went out to buy me some other clothes, which he didn't like doing, and he had to knock at a shop till they unlocked it, and they were giving him as many as he'd got money with him to buy, when they saw a policeman on the other side of the road, and they thought they were being trapped into breaking the law, and they were rude about it and turned him out. So he had to come back to me to explain that people can do anything else at night because it doesn't help other people for it to be done then. They might even have cleaned the shop windows, and the policeman wouldn't have said a word, but they mustn't sell anything, because—well, perhaps you could put it in a way that would make it sound sense better than he was able to do."

"I don't know why you should expect me to make it sound sense. It is a fact that a carpenter or bricklayer can work lawfully at any hour of the day or night, and that it is of no direct advantage to the community for him to work at late hours, though the sum of his industry must be beneficial to them. It is also a fact that it would be of direct benefit to the community for shopkeepers to serve them at all hours, and that they are forbidden to do so. But this is not done at the wish of the general body of the community, whom it inconveniences, as you rightly observe. It is the majority of the shopkeepers who do not wish to work, and who have appealed successfully to the nation to prevent others from doing so."

Elya looked puzzled for a moment, and then said: "It's a beautiful tale. It shows how kind-hearted people are."

"I'm afraid it was less simple than that. The retail trades are well organised. But I am sure that, now you are—now that you have got what you required—you cannot be keenly interested in the legislation to which you have directed such discriminating attention. I wonder whether you would do me the honour of dining with me this evening—just a small party in my room?"

"Yes, of course. I was hoping you'd ask me something like that. I suppose Rodney can come?"

"I shall be pleased if Mr. Surrell will be able to join us."

"Oh, he'll do that! If you watch him you'll see that he's so fond of me that he'll follow anywhere that I go." She turned to her companion to ask: "Isn't that how you feel, Rodney? I shouldn't like to tell Sir Eden anything wrong."

"It has been a great pleasure for us to be together. I should like to think that it may also have been pleasant for you."

"Oh, you can think that," she replied lightly; and then added more seriously: "When we sat on the tree, and you looked at me the way that you did, I had such a queer feeling inside that I had to turn back into a dog as quickly as I could think. I knew we'd got to get on, and I wasn't sure that you might not be forgetting that."

Without appearing to have observed this remarkable statement, Sir Eden said affably: "Well then, we will expect to meet later," put his cigar back into its customary position, and turned away.

Elya said approvingly: "He's got plenty of words; and more sense than you'd expect him to have."

Sir Eden Mountford, having heard the division bell, had hurried back into the House. While he was locked up with his supporters in the "aye" compartment, he spoke to Lady Lucie Channing, the member for Blixworth South. "Lucie," he asked, "are you free to join a little supper party this evening? Just ourselves, and two young people who may be worth knowing. And if you run across Sir Andrew Weyleigh—he's having tea on the terrace now— you might ask him to join us, which I think he'll be willing to do. But don't ask him so that Nixon— Nixon can hear. Tell him that's why I didn't ask him a few minutes ago. You know how touchy Nixon is, and I don't want a big party."

"Is it permissible to ask who the young people are?"

"Yes. But you won't be much wiser; and I want you to come with an open mind. They're both strangers to me. The man seems to be a good sort, and the girl's either a marvel, or else she's a clever fraud."

"And you want me to say which?"

"I should be interested to have your opinion. I haven't got one of my own; but Sir Andrew seems to take her seriously, and he's not easily fooled. And whatever you're thinking, it's quite wrong. The only certain thing is that we shan't be dull."

CHAPTER EIGHTEEN

DINNER FOR FIVE

Lady Lucie was an asset to the party to which she belonged. She had charm. She had wit. She was an incisive speaker at the right times. She had also the capacity to talk for an hour without saying anything, which is an art denied some politicians who are gifted in simpler ways.

She liked the prime minister's dinner parties, which were usually small and select. The conversation could be kept to one subject, and, if there were five present, you could be sure of an audience of four, which is far from being the case at larger gatherings. And when Lady Lucie spoke, she liked to have the attention of those around her.

Now she sat at Sir Eden's right hand, and opposite to her was a young lady of intriguing loveliness, and a cool detachment which suggested that she was either very sure of her own position, or too stupid to appreciate that of her host.

Almost certainly a foreigner. This had been shown by the quaint, if not rude remark which she had made when they had been introduced, "Lady Lucie? It must be nice to be called that. You don't have to wonder whether you are one or not. Or perhaps you do, all the same?"

It had been said in such a tone that it would not have been easy to take offence, but it was not a remark that an Englishwoman would be likely to make, and it was one that reflection did not approve. But, if she were foreign, to what nation did she belong? It was not easy to guess.

She was unmarried, if that question could be resolved by a ringless hand. She wore no jewellery whatever. Her dress was English enough, and unobtrusively good. No one wore evening dress, which the occasion did not allow.

But Lady Lucie thought she knew almost everyone worth knowing, besides a few of whom she was less than sure. And such beauty would not go unobserved. Certainly a foreigner. But why had Sir Eden not been more explicit?

Sir Andrew sat at her right hand, and a Mr. Surrell, whom she certainly had not met before, between him and Elya, completing the circle. Their host had been rather more communicative when introducing him: "He can tell us something of Moscow, but he is one of whom the Russian Embassy does not approve."

There was a hint of international politics here which probably explained everything. He had been in Moscow—probably spying—and had got away with a Russian girl, who might be all she professed, or a spy herself, which was to be probed.

She approved of Surrell's looks. A man, she thought, whom you could trust. And not one to be easily duped. But she knew the guile of women to surpass the defences of the average masculine mind.

Anyway, the premier's hint was sufficient to show her how the conversation could be opened, which she must not defer to do.

She addressed Elya, who was putting strawberry jam on her plate from a full spoon: "I expect you can speak Russian as well as English, Miss Gabriel?"

It was boldly guessed, but on such points Lady Lucie was seldom wrong.

Elya answered in the language mentioned: "Yes, I was in the Russian Embassy yesterday. I bit a man in the neck."

It was a reply which caused Rodney to have a fear that she was going to be indiscreet again, and the prime minister (who knew two languages well, and several others badly) to grasp her meaning enough to hope the same thing.

Knowing nothing of Russian, Lady Lucie was not similarly informed. She continued her exploration. "I expect you know several languages well?"

Elya, who intended to keep her promise to Rodney, and had mischievously relied on Lady Lucie's ignorance of the language, replies merely: "Yes."

But Sir Eden had no such inhibition. He added: "I understand that Miss Gabriel can speak Chinese, and Spanish, and French, and one or two others, equally well."

Lady Lucie showed natural surprise. Miss Gabriel looked young for such erudition. And not the type. She said politely: "You must have spent a long time in acquiring such an extensive variety of difficult tongues."

Elya wished to give a truthful reply. But how long *had* it been? It had been outside the solar system, and the count of days did not apply. The assimilation of so many hundreds of thousands of words really had taken a considerable time. They must be taken in singly, however rapid the process. She was merely trying to be truthful, and to avoid a form of reply which would confuse the inquisitor when she said: "There were a great many words to learn. It must have taken nearly a week."

Lady Lucie was aware of the insult of being told to mind her own business in the form of a flippant lie. She was tempted to a sarcastic answer. But she was too well-bred to brawl at Sir Eden's table. And, besides, had he not asked her to study this foreign woman, about whom he must suspect something he did not trust or approve. She laughed as she replied: "You won't expect me to take that seriously, unless each day means a year."

"Oh, but I did. I tried to calculate just what it had been. I never tell lies. I think you all go to too much trouble in doing that."

"Really, Miss Gabriel, that isn't a very polite thing to say. We may not be in the habit of telling lies any more than yourself." She was tempted to add: "or as much," but again politeness controlled her words.

"You all tell lies," Elya answered calmly. "Even Rodney tells lies to me. He doesn't mean to, but it's a habit he can't break. It's all lies and laws here. If you stopped telling lies and making laws, you'd have nothing to do."

Was it a deliberate insult to Sir Eden and herself in their high vocation? It certainly had that sound, but it should still be taken without offence. She asked: "Do you object to laws also, or is that our redeeming feature?"

"Laws don't matter to me. Except closing shops. But shan't you ever have had enough?"

"Surely, Miss Gabriel, you don't deny that laws are necessary? Without them people could do just what they like."

"And you think they wouldn't like that?"

"They wouldn't like what others would do to them."

Elya recognised in a truthful mind that she had under-estimated the complexity of the problem. She said: "You mean they wouldn't like doing what they like so much as they'd dislike others doing what they liked to them? It sounds a bit difficult to believe, but if that's how it is I don't wonder you all look tired. But Leonard told me that you've got more laws now than anyone understands. Don't you think they may be more than enough?"

"The arrears of legislation," Lady Lucie replied, "are extremely serious. And, I am sorry to say, those of the administration of justice also. Recent parliaments have recognised this evil so acutely that they have delegated a large proportion of law-making to those who have more time than themselves, and many thousands of laws are made by officials in that way. And they have also attempted to relieve—or, at least, not to augment—the congestion of the courts of law by enacting that such laws must be obeyed without question, even of their interpretation. People must learn to obey without argument or appeal."

"You mean," Sir Andrew was tempted to interpose, "that if the Board of Trade says that you mustn't export Chaucer, because *Canterbury Tales* are New Zealand lamb, you can't take the matter before an impartial judge?"

"You know it wouldn't say anything so absurd."

"It has made some rulings about equally silly. But you mean you save time by not allowing the judges to interfere?"

"It certainly saves time, and with the complications of modern life— Yes, it certainly does more good than harm."

"Well, I'm glad my department can have no such responsibility thrown upon it."

"Or wouldn't," Rodney asked, speaking for the first time, "irresponsibility be a better word?"

"It seems to me," Elya said, "that you've all gone mad through starting something you can't stop. I've told you that the only sensible thing to do is to get rid of most of the laws, and understand those that you keep on, but you don't seem able to even think of it seriously. I'm glad London isn't my home address."

"Where do you come from, Miss Gabriel?" Lady Lucie asked politely.

"You wouldn't believe," she replied briefly, wishing that the subject were raised less frequently.

Sir Andrew undertook a more affirmative answer. "Miss Gabriel," he said, "has explained to us that she is an angel incarnate in a human body. It is an assertion which rouses natural surprise. Indeed, incredulity might be a more appropriate word. But she has demonstrated both to Mr. Surrell and myself that it is more than a groundless claim."

Lady Lucie said bluntly: "Incredulity certainly sounds the right word to me. How do you say she's done that?"

"She has transformed herself into various quadrupeds, and on one occasion—by the way, how many legs has a flea?"

"You're not asking me to believe that?"

"I'm not asking you to believe anything. You asked a question, to which I merely gave a truthful reply."

"Then perhaps she'll show us what she can do now. How about being a dog, Miss Gabriel? It isn't I, it's Sir Andrew who suggests that you might like to show yourself to us as a bull-terrier bitch."

Elya looked at the speaker in a quietly contemplative manner, which she found it hard to sustain with the composure that she desired. "If you thought you were being rude," she said serenely, "it was a mistake. We're both bitches, and it's what we prefer to be. But I don't see why I should. And, besides, I'm rather tired of being a dog."

"I was hoping," Sir Eden said, "that we might be privileged to witness a demonstration."

"I'd do it for you, Sir Eden, only I've promised Rodney I won't unless I'm in a bad jam. And, besides, there's always the trouble about the clothes. But for that," she added, looking at Lady Lucie closely, "I mightn't mind being a flea."

But Lady Lucie did not appear to take the remark personally. "I've always wanted," she said, "to watch a performing flea."

"You mightn't like the way that I should perform."

"I have learnt," Sir Andrew explained, "that Miss Gabriel as a flea has a strong bite."

"It doesn't seem to me," Lady Lucie replied, "to be a very good joke."

"It isn't a joke at all, and I'd love to do it. But it isn't only the trouble about the clothes. Rodney really wants me to give up doing anything of the kind. He's heard of someone who had a wife who used to turn into a cat, and jump out of the window just at the moment when he most didn't want her to go. Of course, I shouldn't do anything mean like that, but you can see how he feels."

"It is a contingency," Sir Eden agreed, "against which we were all warned when we were young. But if the difficulty regarding the clothes be what I suppose, it should not be beyond our ingenuity to overcome. Lady Lucie, I am less than fully informed upon the conveniences which our lady members enjoy, but would it not be within the limit of possibilities to provide accommodation for Miss Gabriel to resume her clothing where she would not be subject to oversight or intrusion?"

But Elya did not hear the confident reply that this could easily be arranged in a responsive mood. She felt no desire to be a bull-terrier bitch for Lady Lucie to pat or feed. She turned the conversation back to her favourite theme of redundant laws, and Lady Lucie rose to the bait, as she had done before.

She was led to defend the practice of allowing officials to make laws of their own, which it became the duty of those concerned to discover, and then obey.

She illustrated her argument from her own experience. She had a country house at Chelford-Boscott, to which she resorted at weekends, and when Parliament was not sitting. Here she kept pigs, which could not fulfil their destiny unless they were slaughtered at appropriate times. For that purpose they had to be sent to an address eighteen miles away. That was a regulation. Even she, who (ignoring the pigs) was most nearly concerned, did not know why this should be necessary. But so it was. Would Miss Gabriel propose that the time of the Mother of Parliaments should be wasted on such details as these?

Elya listened with an enjoyment which she made no effort to disguise. It was a weird insanity surpassing anything she had heard before. But she became graver as she remarked: "It must be a long walk for the pigs."

"They don't walk," Lady Lucie replied impatiently. (Was there no limit to the ignorance of this silly woman?) "They go in carts."

"But that must cost money. I know everything else does."

"It costs something, of course."

"Then why don't you refuse to pay it? They couldn't go without that. Unless the man who made the law paid for them himself. And if you want another law, wouldn't that be a very good one to make—that every man paid for his own laws, so that they'd have to stop when his money'd gone?"

"That," Sir Eden interposed to explain, "already happens in a remote way so far as those which are made in parliament are concerned, because the whole community is responsible (or, at least, a majority of them) and they must all finally pay. But so far as those who are delegated to make compulsory regulations are concerned, I am afraid they would decline to make them on so onerous a condition."

This remark had the unusual effect of reducing Elya to a momentary silence, not because it left her barren either of thoughts or words, but because their plurality was their own undoing.

She was astonished, even after all she had heard before, that the cost of a law should be borne equally by those who opposed or approved it. It was such a fundamental inequity! And how absurd it was to say that officials would not make laws for which they themselves must pay, when all that was required was to make another law to compel them to do so!

She saw that, when it has once been accepted that men have the right to interfere with their neighbours' private affairs, there can be no logical limit at which such tyranny can be barred. But hadn't she heard something about people being certified as insane, and might there not be a remedy there? *Non compos mentis*; those were the magic words which had fallen from Laura's lips, and she had liked their sound from the first. She must learn Latin when she had a few moments to spare. It might have other illuminations for lively minds. But Sir Eden was speaking again, and when he spoke he always had something to say.

"You should know," he said, "that Lady Lucie is not only one of our legislators, she deals with law from another angle. She is Chairman of the Magistrates at Chelford-Boscott, and I have been told that her judgements have never been overset on appeal."

He spoke in random kindness, having a feeling that Lady Lucie was being somewhat roughly handled in the investigation that he had asked her to make. He wished both to restore her equanimity, and to turn the conversation back to more dramatic possibilities. But its effect was to bring a sudden light of mischief to Elya's eyes. It was an audacious, delightful thought, but could it—or how best could it—be done?

She said: "I don't know where Chelford-Boscott is. I've never been outside London, except when Leonard took me to Godalming, and we only stayed there for a few hours. Is it worth going to see?"

Rodney saw a chance which he must not miss. He said quickly: "It's in Buckinghamshire. It's a lovely spot. I once stayed the night there at the Red Bull—one of the Truscott hotels. You can always depend on them. I'll show it you any day, if you'd like the run."

"That," Elya replied, in a happy excitement she had no care to conceal, "is just what I meant to propose. But any day wouldn't do. I like to do things properly. I know it has to be the weekend. And I ought to tell someone that I'm going to see a grandmother, or an old aunt. But I can't do that. You'd better write for a double room, and say you're bringing your wife."

When a man receives a public proposal from the girl he intends to marry for an informal weekend together, his reaction may be difficult to foretell. Rodney was conscious of some confusion of mind. But they all knew that Elya was not—well, not quite of a conventional type. He said: "Well, that's for you to say."

"I should think it is! And it's for you to look pleased. If I'd given Sir Andrew the chance, he'd have taken it in a different way. Wouldn't you, Sir Andrew? I'm not sure that I shan't change, even now."

But her words were as casual as the invitation itself had been. She hardly heard Sir Andrew's adroit reply that he should expect to be murdered by Mr. Surrell before

Saturday would arrive, for her thoughts were on other things.

CHAPTER NINETEEN

MAGISTRATES' COURT

"I can get a special license, and we can be married on Thursday."

"I don't think we could, even if I should agree, which is asking for a lot more than you're ever likely to get."

"What's the difficulty?"

"You find they'd be about fifty. I'm not English. What should you do about that? And I haven't got a father, nor any age. Those things mightn't matter. I suppose a few extra lies would leave the total about the same. But you'd want me to start telling them when we should get to the registrar, and I never do. Don't you know that the marriage service is *all* lies, from start to end? Anyway, I'm not going to do it. I shall go to the Red Bull, and if I find you've booked for me, it will be all the better for you. But if you'd rather go to Lady Lucie, I suppose it will be all the better for her."

"Lady Lucie is a married woman, more likely than not."

"I should say it's more likely she's a widow. She'd wear any man out in three weeks—or perhaps four."

"Do you call that telling the truth?"

"There's about as much truth as you can get into that number of words. But I don't mind if not. I want to learn how to tell lies, and practice must be the best way. Only I couldn't begin by telling a lot all at once; and the marriage service goes on as though it would never stop."

"Very well. You shall have it your own way. I'll wire for a room at the Red Bull, and we'll go down together."

"Then I'll kiss you for saying that." Which she proceeded to do.

It followed from this conversation that, in the early hours of the following Sunday morning, Rodney lay in the double bed of a moonlit room, and was disturbed in his well-earned rest by stealthy movement and slightest sound sufficiently to put out his arm to give redundant embrace to a body which was not there. Awakened further by this negation, he was dimly aware of the hind legs and lifted tail of a cat which was leaving the open window for the insecurity of an ivied wall.

He lay still. It was not a dream. On the data which he already had it was an incident reasonably to have been foreseen. He resolved to lie awake to await her return. But such resolutions may not be easy to keep. Elya had much to do and to learn. She was also delayed by the presence, at an essential point, of an amorous cat to whom she did not wish to respond. It was in the twilight of a daylight-saving four-thirty that she returned, and crept quietly into the welcome warmth of a bed where her partner slept, which (at that time) was what she wished him to do.

On Sunday night she was absent again, and on Monday she yawned. But she was in high spirits, and Rodney knew her well enough now to guess that mischief was in her mind, though he had no remotest conception of what it would be likely to be, even when she showed extreme curiosity concerning the municipal building, dignified by the name of Council House. This stood almost opposite to the Red Bull, and contained, *inter alia*, a small assembly room in which, on alternate Tuesdays, the local magistrates were accustomed to dispense justice, under the discreet guidance of Mr. Archibald Sipsoup (Sipsoup, Handel & Sipsoup), a sound lawyer, a man of cold but impartial severity, and who regarded the human race as existing mainly that they might obey and be chastised by the law that he feared and loved.

She had learned much in conversations with the caretaker, the town clerk, three constables, the municipal treasurer, the court usher, and a rate collector's assistant, on all of whom she had bestowed her radiant presence, and left them bewildered men.

Rodney had been well content with her suggestion that a weekend does not necessarily terminate before Tuesday evening, but learnt, with qualified surprise, as they shared a good dinner on Monday before attending the Odeon Cinema, that she had arranged a programme for the following day in which his performance was not required.

"I expect," she said, "you'll find I'm gone when you wake tomorrow, and you mayn't see me again till it's time for us to go back. If I'm not back before five—but I shall be, more likely than not—you'd better pay the bill, and just wait till I come in, ready to go. I shall do most of my packing tonight."

"Am I to understand that we may have to move quickly when you appear?"

"I don't see why we should. But I always have to remember you're not easy to get away, and I never want you to use your guns."

"I had no such thought in my mind. I hope you haven't been examining the courtroom so closely because you expect to have to get me out of the dock?"

"No, I wasn't thinking of that. I haven't been thinking of you at all. I'm hoping to do some good. But it's being troublesome to arrange, and unless it turns out to be lots of fun—"

"Is it anything in which I could assist? I mean, when you stop being a cat."

"Oh, you've noticed that? No, I don't think there is. And I'm *sick* of being a cat. Besides that I'm not sure that it's quite safe. Suppose I were a cat, and got my leg caught in a spring trap, would it still be caught if I changed back?"

"It is a problem on which your opinion should be of more value than mine."

"So it should. And I expect it would be all right. But I'm rather frightened that I don't know."

"Is it an eventuality which there may be reason to fear?"

"Not especially. But there's a case on at the court tomorrow. It just made me think."

"But I can't be of any assistance to you in whatever you're up to now?"

"No. I don't see how you can. But you can come to court tomorrow. I hope you'll think it worthwhile. Lady

Lucie is on the bench, and only one magistrate with her. He's a Mr. Thompson. He'll be no trouble at all."

"May I conclude that you intend to be there?"

"You can look round for me, but I hope it won't do any good."

"Well, I suppose I must wait, and see what happens. You are fairly good at looking after yourself."

"Yes, I think I am. And I like to feel you're ready to help. But you're quite wrong if you think I want to have any upset there. It's Lady Lucie you'll need to watch."

Finding that he must be content with this cryptic prophecy, Rodney left the future to take care of itself, and went on to introduce his celestial *amie* to the temple of modern art, where he had the benefit of some expert criticisms on the figure of Ginger Rogers, which that talented actress was fortunate that she did not hear.

He was not surprised when he waked next morning to find that he was alone, and after breakfasting, and becoming conscious thereby of how much he missed the conversation of his fluctuant lover, he walked over to the courthouse, where, as he had been told to expect, Lady Lucie Channing was presiding, with a rather vacuous-eyed gentleman beside her, middle-aged, with a sagging mouth, and fast-thinning hair, whom he correctly supposed to be the Mr. Thompson of whom it had been foretold that he would be "no trouble at all." But what kind of trouble would he not be likely to be?

Seated singly at a lower table was Mr. Sipsoup, the power behind or below, but also above the throne, to whose rigid legality it may be attributed that Lady Lucie's decisions had so invariably had the support of the higher courts, when those to whom they had involved injustice had been perverse enough to appeal against them.

He was speaking now, with mechanical suavity, but in a voice which, though low-pitched, was penetratingly bleak and hard.

It was the preliminary half hour during which applications could be made to the bench. Now a solicitor put a form before him, to which he nodded assent, and passed it up to Lady Lucie to sign, which, after a moment's perusal, she did, and passed it back to him.

Rodney, alert for the unexpected, noticed that the solicitor looked at the signature with puzzled eyes, and then—had it not been signed in his own presence?—put it into his briefcase and left the court. But there could be no importance in that.

The solicitor had thought the signature to be unlike that which he was accustomed to get, but had he known even half of that which the lady had undergone since daylight came, he might have been more surprised that she should be able to sign at all.

She had been awakened much earlier than her habit was by the irritation caused by an industrious flea, which—or should we say who?—had been marking her in the pattern of an opprobrious word which it—or she—had been unable to bring to a satisfactory end.—And after that she had gone through the worst horror her life had known.

A gigantic Negro—or perhaps Negress, for the monster was clothed only in her own dressing gown, which left its black knees bare—had seized her roughly, and when she had thought herself destined to be either raped or murdered, or more probably both, and had been too terrified even to scream, had merely trussed her up in a most un-dignified way, and left her too securely bound and blinded and gagged to be aware that the person was no longer visible, and a young woman with a figure which Aphrodite would have been thankful to have, but a face which was like her own, was searching among her clothes for anything which such a figure would be able to wear.

There can be no pleasure in observing the weakness of one who comes from supernal realms, but truth is a goddess to be obeyed. Elya, with more trouble than she expected to have, had contrived for herself a face exactly resembling that which Lady Lucie Channing was accustomed to show the world. We know it to have been far from a bad face, but it was one which Elya disliked. Only the delight of the audacity she proposed could reconcile her to the degradation which she thought it to be. But Lady Lucie's figure—no, it simply could not be done. We know that consciousness of the female figure was Elya's feature, if not her fault.

But having reduced her victim to immobility, she descended to breakfast, to amaze a parlour maid with the vigour of her movements, and an appetite which Lady Lucie had never known.

The car was at the door at the usual time, and without arousing suspicion of that which is clearly beyond belief, she was soon looking down on a court room which, for one day at least, would be docile to do her will.

Rodney, watching for any sign of the presence of one he felt sure was not far away, heard the cross-summonses of Beddoes and Tomkins called. Mr. Sipsoup turned up his face to Lady Lucie, who leaned over to him. For a time they whispered together, and then she became upright again, and announced in a surprisingly clear and resonant voice, that the two summonses would be taken together. Upon which Mr. Ripton, solicitor to Mr. Amos Beddoes, rose to address the court.

The facts, it appeared, were not in dispute, though the parties' intentions were. Mr. Beddoes' cat had been caught in a rabbit-trap set by Percy Tomkins, and its leg had been broken, with the sequel that it had been destroyed by a veterinary surgeon in humanity's name. Amos had thrown the trap, and two others which he had found set under the same hedge, into a river from which they could not easily be retrieved. He had done more than that. He had torn up nine others which were set in a further hedge, and hurled them to the same fate.

His contention was that the three which had been set in the first hedge had not been intended for rabbits at all, it being one which no sane man would have selected for their undoing, but that they had been planted with the express purpose of catching his cat, on a track which it was accustomed to use. He said that Tomkins disliked the cat because it took rabbits which he preferred to catch for his own use.

He contended that the outrage justified his action in uprooting traps which had been put to so lawless a use, and he claimed two pounds as the value of the dead cat. There was a haystack near his cottage, which was the home of numerous rats, and it had been the cat's essential service to scare them away.

Mr. Witherspoon, the solicitor representing Tomkins, an older and quieter man than the eloquent Ripton, replied that he was content to let the facts speak for themselves; with the leave of the court, he proposed to put in a plan of the land.

Elya had come to enjoy herself, as her habit was, but she also wished to do good. Beyond that, she wished to administer the law in effective ways.

Now she consulted her colleagues politely, and then said that they would be pleased to admit the plan, but would like to know first that its accuracy would be admitted by both parties. It appeared that Percy must have had some money to spend, for it now spread out beyond the width of the solicitors' table, and while Amos and Mr. Ripton were leaning over it, Elya lent forward to Mr. Sipsoup to garner legal wisdom from its usual source.

She found it to be a case which provided no difficulties for him, even before the witnesses had been called. Unless it could be shown (which had not been claimed) that Tomkins had set the traps beyond the limit of his own land, it was futile to suggest that he had an intention which was beyond proof, and which he would be sure to deny. On the other hand, to destroy or immerse another man's property is beyond legal defence. The claim against Tomkins should be dismissed, and Amos should be ordered to pay for the traps, for which £4.3.0. had been claimed. But they were probably rusty and old. Why not give judgement for £3.10.0.? Beddoes might be fined also. But that need not be much. He had naturally been annoyed that his cat had been injured. And, of course, there would be costs against him.

Elya would have liked to get it over quickly, for she knew that two other cases would follow, if there should be time to hear them, which were likely to give more amusement to her. But there was an aspect of the matter which she felt should not be put lightly aside. She said: "It's the man who killed the cat who ought to be here."

Mr. Sipsoup made no reply. He knew that Lady Lucie did not often make silly remarks, and he did not wish to appear dense. But what possible charge could there be against the veterinary surgeon? Or what need for his evidence, unless it should be alleged that the cat's leg had not been broken at all? But they were now agreed upon the accuracy of the plan, and Amos Beddoes was in the box.

The plan proved that Percy had set the traps well within his own territory, but Amos did not dispute that, and, apart from that, his contention had an aspect of probability. Percy had a garden which was protected by a high brick wall, which no rabbit would climb. Outside the wall was a footpath, there being a right of way through his land. On the other side of the path was the hedge under which the three traps had been set. Beyond that was an arable field, also owned by him, now cropped with potatoes, and then a sandy bank, with rabbit burrows, and the further hedge, where the other nine traps had been more sensibly placed.

There was a gate in Percy's wall which could be scaled by an active cat, and this Amos's cat had been seen to do. It was opposite to this gate, where there was a narrow trodden path under the hedge, that the fatal trap had been set.

Amos defended his treatment of the traps, not only through indignation at his cat's injury, but on more general grounds. "They're beastly things," he said, "as ought not to be used."

Mr. Witherspoon did not cross-examine him. He considered that he had condemned himself, and there was no need for a further wasting of words.

But Elya had a few questions to ask.

"Mr. Beddoes, will you tell the court why you paid someone to kill the cat?"

The man stared and hesitated at this unexpected question. Then he gave a literal answer, "Because he wouldn't 'a' done it for nowt."

"But why have it done at all?"

"To put the poor beast outa 'er misery."

"You mean it wasn't to save yourself trouble, or some expense? It was sympathy for the cat?"

The man looked down, shuffling his feet. He looked round the court, as though seeking rescue from a persecution he did not deserve. Then he said: "It's what us all does."

Mr. Ripton rose. "I think what my client means is that, under such circumstances, it is the normal practice to put the poor animal out of its misery as quickly as possible. He would, of course, have been entitled to destroy his own cat in a humane manner under any circumstances, but with the injury that it had there was really no other course."

"There was an obvious alternative. Your client has said that he was led to make away with the traps because he disliked their cruelty. In weighing the genuineness of this plea, it is relevant to observe his conduct to his own cat."

"Then I can only submit, your worship, that he acted in the manner which is customary under such circumstances, and is commonly regarded as most humane."

He was surprised that Lady Lucie should question that, and concluded that she must be a cat lover who could not give unbiased judgement where those animals were concerned. That was unfortunate for his client. And yet, was that certain? Might not Tomkins have incurred her heavier reprobation? And (with Sipsoup's help) she could be relied upon for a level-headed judgement more often than not. He decided to say no more. And, surprisingly, Elya came to the same decision. She had been tempted to ask the witness what he would wish done if his own leg were broken, and then, if he gave the logical answer, to ask his neighbours to remember what he had said. But she had a well-timed thought that there would almost certainly be a law against killing a man, even at his publicly expressed desire, and it was one which Lady Lucie would be almost certain to know. Of course, he could kill himself under such circumstances, but there might even be a law against *that*! To imagine a limit to human silliness was almost certainly to guess wrong. And now Percy was in the box.

Mr. Witherspoon asked him few questions in a manner which suggested that his case was too strong for it to be worth the labour of many words. He treated it as though the only question at issue were the value of stolen traps, and his client gave brief but sufficient replies.

But when Mr. Ripton rose to cross-examine, the atmosphere changed. Questions were sharp, and Percy became aggressive in his replies. Could he not set his traps where he would on his own land? Was he responsible for the safety of trespassing cats? It led nowhere, and Mr. Ripton had the sense to drop it and let it go. Or, at least, he would have been permitted to do so had not Elya asked him one further question. "Mr. Tomkins," she said, in her kindliest manner, "have you ever been certified as insane, or placed in a mental home?"

"No, your worship," he answered angrily. "I reckon I'm as sane as any man here. Or woman either."

"I wonder," she said, with a considering smile, "whether that could have been meant for me? But I don't think, Mr. Tomkins, that your friends have looked after you as they ought to have done. Mr. Witherspoon, if your client really set those three traps to catch rabbits, it is a clear case of *non compos mentis*" (how she blessed Laura for that resonant phrase), "and it may be in his own interest for you to consider the matter from that angle."

But no solicitor, in the absence of such instructions, will be quick to plead that his client has lost his wits, and Mr. Witherspoon continued the skirmish on more conventional lines. He addressed the court on his client's behalf. Mr. Ripton did the same. Law books were quoted, and there were animated discussions between the two and Mr. Sipsoup, while Elya concealed a yawn.

But all things come to an end at last (or, at least, that has been the experience of the human race to the present day), and the time came when Elya, having first turned sideways to consult her unspeaking colleague, and then leaned over to treat Mr. Sipsoup with a similar courtesy, gave the judgement of the court.

"So far," she said, "as the case of Beddoes v. Tomkins is concerned, there is not much which it could be useful to say. If the three traps were set for the purpose of catching rabbits, as the defendant has sworn, he was insane, and the plea of insanity has not been raised, judgement must be given against him. He intended the trap for Beddoes' cat, with the result that he gave it a broken leg, for which he will be sent to prison…"—she looked hard at Mr. Ripton as she said this—"…for fourteen days. You will not over-look that it may be increased on appeal."

He did not overlook that. He could appeal to quarter sessions, and Lady Lucie would be on the bench. He re-membered that her decisions had never been overruled. He heard the low whisper of another solicitor at his right hand: "You'll let it ride, if you're a wise man." So he would.

Elya was feeling hungry. She looked at the clock. It was rather early for lunch, but rather late for starting an-other case—and a more important one than that with which she had dealt. She said the court would adjourn.

She retired to a room which was reserved for the use of Lady Lucie on these occasions. Lunch would be sent over to her from the Red Bull. She felt quietly happy. She had done some good, though the man who set those snares (how easily it might have been she!) had escaped too lightly. But her moral code was not law, though she might have some frisky ways, and she would not punish him for that which it had been legal to do. But to think of all the thousands of laws there were—insolent, tyrannical, bully-ing, thieving, snooping, vexatious laws—and not one to forbid the use of such traps as that! And she had guessed that Ripton would be influenced by the belief that she would be present at quarter sessions. Could she not hope that she might really be learning to lie?

CHAPTER TWENTY

LADY LUCIE ACHIEVES FAME

Elya looked into a gilt full-mirror of ancient pattern as she picked a crumb from her sleeve, with the fastidious care that she had learned to observe in celestial halls. Even the sight of a face which she had had no willingness to assume could not ruffle the surface of a mind which was aware of good deeds accomplished and others nearly ahead. The thought of Lady Lucie lying trussed up on her own bed, with a notice "DO NOT DISTURB" thoughtfully pinned to the bedroom door, would have been sufficient of itself to explain the dimple which enhanced the beauty of her left cheek. And then for thirty seconds she was disturbed by the realisation of what (she would have said) was the first blunder that she had made. There had been two summonses, and she had delivered judgement on one only, although they had been taken together by her own decision. Why hadn't that absolute ass on her left reminded her of that which was his matter as much as hers?

Then her serenity was resumed, as, with her usual mental agility, she saw how the situation might still be handled to its own advantage.

Of one thing she was firmly resolved. Tomkins should not be paid for the traps which had been removed. She had meant that all along, but it was only now that she saw a way by which it could be assured without self-condemnation, or the protests of the gentlemen seated below.

As she was taking her place, she spoke quickly, lest others should be first to mention the oversight which had been hers. "When we adjourned," she said, "I reserved decision upon the cross-summons of Beddoes against Tomkins, with which we must now deal.

"Mr. Witherspoon, I have a suggestion to make, which, in your client's interests, may be worth your consideration. There is no doubt that, should the matter be pressed, Amos Beddoes is liable for an action which, however much it may win the sympathy of decent people, has no legal defence. But if your client should show sufficient consciousness of the moral issues involved to withdraw the summons, I should be disposed to grant him bail until the next sitting of the court, when I might do no more than bind him over, if, after that period of reflection, he should be prepared to give an undertaking to make no effort to reclaim the lost traps, or to use others of a similar kind."

Mr. Witherspoon hesitated. He did not like the offer, which outraged his sense of legal propriety, and he could see, by the expression on the face of the magistrates' clerk, that he was appalled by that against which it was too late for him to protest. But a client who is in jail will not thank his solicitor if he rejects an offer of his release. He said doubtfully: "I am bound to observe that the use of the traps in question is wholly legal."

Elya smiled in a way which Lady Lucie would have been unlikely to do. "That," she said, "is precisely why I have made you an offer your client does not deserve."

Mr. Witherspoon's next question showed that he was preparing to yield. "I may suppose that the amount of bail would not be prohibitive?"

"His own recognisance would be all that would be required."

"Then I will take the responsibility of withdrawing the summons."

Elya was conscious of satisfaction such as mortals can seldom feel. She had disposed of the matter in what she felt to be an equitable manner with little support from a law which had failed to function in spite of all its *redundancies*, she had disposed of it quickly, which was of importance to her, there being two other cases with which it would be a pleasure to deal, for which time was becoming provokingly short, and she had done so in such a way that it would come before Lady Lucie in a fortnight's time, when it would be difficult for her, without incredible assertion, to criticise what had apparently been done by herself before. And now Mr. Rumpkin-Rumpkin Q.C. was rising, and Mrs. Ada Levinson, a large-nosed woman, vulgarly but expensively dressed, whose Bentley waited outside the court, was being shown into the dock.

But it appeared that her solicitor, now in whispering conference with Mr. Sipsoup on her behalf, was objecting to this. Could not the wealthy lady be accommodated with a seat before it?

Mr. Sipsoup saw no objection to this. He looked up to Elya for confirmation. Mrs. Levinson was now standing uncertainly in the ignominious enclosure. Elya said: "No, why should she? I can see her better where she is now. But why doesn't she sit down?"

"She is waiting," Mr. Sipsoup replied, in an audible whisper, "for your permission." He had wondered more than once during the morning whether Lady Lucie might be unwell.

"Mrs. Levinson," Elya said, "you've no reason to stand like that. It's contempt of court to suppose that I'm silly enough to object to anyone sitting down."

Mrs. Levinson was in an unhappy position. She was a neighbour and acquaintance of Lady Lucie, and had vaguely hoped that this might have been of some advantage to her. Now she looked at one who showed no sign of recognition, and who insisted that she should enter the dock. There might possibly be some indication of favour in the queer wording of the permission to sit, but it was not easy to think.

Now Mr. Rumpkin-Rumpkin was stating the case against her with a lucidity which was no pleasure for her to hear. It appeared that she had landed from a cross-channel boat wearing a coat of mink which had naturally attracted the notice of the Customs officers, who had declined to accept, without confirmation, her assertion that she had bought it in London ten years previously. Although she had declared all other dutiable articles in her luggage with punctilious exactness, they had detained the coat, while giving her an opportunity to prove its origin.

"This being the position," the learned counsel continued, "the defendant forwarded to the Customs Office a document purporting to be a receipt for £3,200 paid by her to Messrs Stork & Ladwick, the well-known furriers, for a mink coat purchased on October the 22nd 1942, the description of which agreed sufficiently with that of the one which had been detained to give a reasonable expectation that it would be accepted as satisfactory evidence of origin. But the defendant may not have been aware that the Customs authorities have their own channels of information, and, before this receipt was tendered, they had conclusive evidence in their possession that the coat which they had detained was bought from Lateur & Cie of Paris, by a lady with whom Mrs. Levinson was staying, and who apparently acted as an agent on her behalf.

"I regret to have to say that Mrs. Levinson denied this, and has continued to assert that the coat in our possession is the one which she bought in England at the earlier date. We propose therefore to prove its identity, and to ask for an exemplary penalty. The defendant, as I need hardly inform the court, is liable, in addition to the forfeiture of the coat in question, to a penalty equal to three times its value, which I shall ask you to impose commensurately to the nature of the offence which has been committed."

Mr. Rumpkin-Rumpkin certainly had not finished his opening speech. He merely paused, either for breath or effect, at the end of a sonorous period, but Elya took advantage of the second's silence to say: "You can get a good flat for less than ten pounds a week. I don't see how a fur coat can be worth more than twenty pounds, or thirty at the most."

This remark, so reasonable in itself, and yet so far from fact, brought the defendant's counsel, Mr. Coulson Clark, to his feet, and the two barristers spoke at once.

Mr. Rumpkin-Rumpkin said: "The actual amount paid for the coat which we detained was, at the current rate of exchange, £4,003.7.4. The penalty for which the defendant has rendered herself liable is therefore £12,010.2.0."

Mr. Coulson Clark said: "The amount which my client paid for the coat was £3,200, as her receipt conclusively proves."

"It cannot do more," Elya replied patiently to the second of the two speakers, who had only lost by a short head, "than show that Mrs. Levinson did a silly thing. Why not let them keep the coat, which must remind her of what a simpleton she was every time she would put it on, and end a foolish affair amicably?"

"It is a solution which I might see my way to advise my client—," Mr. Coulson Clark began hopefully, but he was interrupted by his opponent's more powerful voice: "It is not an offer which I could possibly accept. A heavy penalty has been incurred, and we must ask for judgement accordingly."

We have observed already that Elya was very far from being a fool, though her inexperience of human values and practices might sometimes lead her astray. She saw that no coat, though it should wear for a lifetime, both day and night, could possibly be worth thousands of pounds; but she also saw that if the number of a certain type of coat should be substantially less than that of the silly women who were anxious to have one of them on their backs, its price could only be limited by the amount of money they had, and the degree of silliness which was theirs—and the supreme silliness of humanity was a matter on which she already had a clear mind. She asked: "Do I understand,

Mr. Rumpkin-Rumpkin, that you seriously value the coat which is in your hands at over four thousand pounds?"

The learned counsel saw that the amount of the penalty that could be claimed depended upon this figure, which he had therefore no reason to depreciate. He said: "Yes, it is a value which can be easily proved."

"Then what do you propose to do with it?"

"As it can be conclusively shown that it is the one which was purchased abroad a few weeks ago, it is clearly forfeit to the Crown."

"That may be the legal position. What I asked was how far you proposed to take advantage of it."

"We regard it as already forfeited."

"Then for whatever wrong Mrs. Levinson may have done you propose that she should be fined over four thousand pounds?"

"It is a risk which she appears to have taken with open eyes."

"Mr. Rumpkin-Rumpkin," Elya replied, in the sweetest voice which could come out of Lady Lucie's mouth, "are you not aware that a direct question should have a direct reply?"

The learned counsel saw that he was not pleasing the court, which is a fault of advocacy, however it may arise.

He said: "Unless my learned friend be prepared to prove that the coat is really the one which was purchased in England some years ago, which I am assured that he will be unable to do, I submit that it is already forfeited, and that the only matter remaining to be decided is the amount of penalty to be inflicted for a persistent attempt to defraud the Customs."

"For which you regard four thousand pounds as an inadequate penalty?"

"It is hardly a question of how I regard it. It is a matter of applying to you to enforce the law."

"But is equity above or under the law? It is to that point that your argument should be addressed. Let me ask you this: if this woman's crime should be considered deserving of so great a penalty that, with four thousand pounds of her property in your hands, you come here to ask that she may be further punished, what should you consider sufficient punishment for a man who should drive to the common danger? Or, shall we say, for someone who would snatch sixpence from a child's hand?"

Mr. Rumpkin-Rumpkin had seldom been asked a question to which he found it more difficult to reply. Not, he would have said, that it was difficult in itself, but because he was mentally confused by the nature of the discussion which was being forced upon him. He had not appeared before Lady Lucie Channing on any previous occasion, and he now thought her to be one who talked at times like a child of ten, and at others would show a subtlety of which the keenest wits should beware. Now he said: "The offences are of such different quality, and may themselves be dependent upon so many relevant circumstances, that it is difficult—"

"Never mind that," Elya interrupted, with a continuance of her sweetest manner, "I didn't expect that you would answer it. Probably no lawyer would. And I'm not sure that it was a fair question to ask, at least, not to ask you. But I think Mr. Coulson Clark has got something to say."

So it was, for, while there had been opportunity, Counsel had consulted his client, and he now rose to say that, if it would dispose of the matter, his client would be prepared, without prejudice, to withdraw her plea that the coat had been purchased in this country, which he was pleased to understand that the court considered—as it well might—was a sufficient penalty for the offence.

"I could not possibly—," Mr. Rumpkin-Rumpkin began. But Elya had looked at the clock. She saw that she must put an end to this case, if she were to have the further pleasure indicated by the legal gentlemen, officials, and witnesses, who were waiting with difficult patience for an innings which it seemed unlikely that they would have. She interrupted in Lady Lucie's most definite manner. "Mr. Rumpkin-Rumpkin, the offer was not addressed to you, but the court. It is not one which I feel should dispose of the matter. You have, I suppose some witnesses here?"

"I have all that can be required."

"That is the point on which we might not agree. Have you the official who is primarily responsible for originating this remarkable action?"

"No, naturally not. That would be—"

"I am not interested in whom it may be. But he must be here at ten-thirty on the next sitting of the court—that is, this day fortnight. For yourself, I can only advise you to surrender a brief which it was an insult to offer to any barrister of repute. You will tell your clients that the issue which must be faced is whether law should override equity, or equity override law. But in saying that I do not wish to be misunderstood. I have no sympathy with the defendant, who has admitted her roguery by the offer which she has made. It is not a case where I can accept her own recognisances. She must remain in custody until she can provide two sureties of £500 each. But a rogue may fall into the hands of others who are stronger than she, which is what Mrs. Levinson appears to have done. Mr. Sipsoup, I think we should go on to the next case, which looks to me as though it should not take long."

Elya leaned back in a happy mood when she had said this. She had no adequate conception of the fame (if that be the correct word) which she would have brought to Lady Lucie Channing when the next morning's newspapers would appear. But she had an impish pleasure in speculating upon how the high official who was to attend next Tuesday week would be received. But if she were going to sit till half past five, or perhaps six, there was one vacancy which must be relieved. "Usher," she said, in a voice which penetrated to the policeman who guarded the furthest door, "will you slip out and get me a bath bun—or perhaps three? You must remind me to give you the money before we leave. Not that it really matters whether you do or not. I never forget anything. But I've left my bag in the room where I have lunch. You'd better put someone to watch the door. Or, better still, bring me the bag. I don't suppose people are honest here. It isn't sense to expect."

CHAPTER TWENTY-ONE

A QUESTION OF DEMOLITION

Buns were going rapidly into Lady Lucie's mouth while a barrister with the simple name of Bird Atkinson was addressing the court. Not that he was a simple man. He was far too eminent to appear frequently in a magistrates' court. In fact, he rarely appeared in any court, high or low.

He advised Councils. Town clerks applied to him for guidance on points of law concerning the obligations of land owners, ancient lights, building restrictions, and rights of way.

He had no forensic ability, which he did not desire. Now, as he addressed the bench, he did not argue, he merely explained. By condescension and courtesy, he would meet the magistrates on their own level. It was a matter between him and themselves, by which a member of the public would be dealt with—well, as they deserve when they give trouble to, or rebel against, those who decide what shall be done.

Mr. John Corbett had built a house. He had done it at his own cost, with his own materials, on his own land.

Through a degree either of ignorance or contumacy hard to believe, *he had not asked the local surveyor to pass the plans.* With a forbearance which must be admired, the representative of law and order had inspected it unasked. Had it conformed to the pattern locally approved, the house might have stood, and the Council's dignity been satisfied by a heavy fine. But he had found that the kitchen ceiling had been two and a half inches too low, and the length of the second bedroom one and three-quarter inches too short. Under such circumstances, there was only one possible course. He applied, on the Council's behalf, for the demolition order which they were entitled to have.

He did not speak as one who argued a doubtful case, but as proceeding in an orderly manner upon an evident path. In formal proof, he put the building surveyor of the Chelford-Boscott District Council into the box.

Elya knew enough of the case already, having had it outlined to her by Mr. Sipsoup, to have decided what must be done, though she had resolved to listen with a patient impartial mind, as an angel may. She would do justice. Her sense of equity would not be quietened by less than that. But she would also have all the fun that she could.

She heard Thomas Fryer sworn, and judged him to be a quiet, sane, respectable man—certainly too small a catch for an angel's net.

She asked him, before the examination commenced: "Are you responsible for the bringing of this action?"

He looked slightly surprised, but answered readily: "No, your worship. I am the Council's surveyor. The action is brought by the Council themselves."

"On your advice?"

"On my report. My advice was not required."

"It was brought perhaps by the building Committee?"

"No. It was by resolution of the Council."

"Unanimously?"

"Yes, I believe so."

"By whom was the resolution moved?"

"By Mr. Telling. He is the chairman of the Building Committee."

"Is he present now?"

"No, I don't see him."

"Does he live near here?"

"I don't know where he lives. He's got an ironmonger's business in Welford St."

"Which is near here? Mr. Atkinson, will you kindly get Mr. Telling to come to the court as quickly as possible?" She looked at the barrister with laughing eyes. "You needn't look as though you're a butler, and someone's told you to cut the grass."

Mr. Atkinson certainly did not show any sign of doing that which had been asked, but the Council's solicitor relieved the position by saying that he would send a clerk to request Mr. Telling's presence, which he proceeded to do.

Mr. Fryer then gave his evidence fairly enough. He had reported to his Committee that the house was being erected without the plans being passed, and they had not been submitted for his inspection. He visited the house, and if it had conformed to his requirements, all might still have been well. He had made a carefully accurate report upon it. The Council had decided that a house which had been built in defiance of their authority, and which did not conform to their requirements, could not be allowed to stand.

Elya decided that he was not one whom it would be seemly to bait. She confined herself to commenting on his final statement: "It is difficult to understand why. But perhaps Mr. Telling can explain that."

So he might have been allowed to withdraw from a publicity which he had not sought, but Mr. Corbett's solicitor had far different views.

He jumped up eagerly with the sharp question: "Mr. Fryer, will you tell the court how many houses there are within the district which you survey?"

"I have never counted them."

"Will you accept that the number is eleven thousand and four?"

Mr. Fryer considered this. Then he said: "I should think you may be about right."

"And that the number of families in the same area is fourteen thousand and twenty-three?"

"I don't know about that. I should have guessed them as more rather than less."

"Then there is a shortage of over three thousand houses?"

"More or less, that may be about it."

"And in such a position you think it's a sensible thing to pull down a house on such pretexts as we have heard?"

Elya heard a voice at her left hand. She had ceased to consider her colleague as anything better than a deaf mute. But he muttered now, "The man's just a dirty rat." She concluded accurately that this description was applied to the solicitor, whom, for whatever reason, Mr. Thompson did not approve.

She saw that the witness was reluctant to answer a question on which he might disagree with that which his employers had done. Anyway, she sought higher game. She said: "Mr. Fryer is here to give us facts, not opinions, which we can form for ourselves."

The solicitor was rebellious. He said: "I protest that my question was quite in order."

Elya replied: "It was quite in order; but it was addressed to the wrong man." She gave Mr. Fryer permission to leave the box. She reflected next moment that she had decided upon assumption rather than fact. Was it because, for no reason known to herself, the man had been called a rat? She spoke frankly: "If it should appear that I am wrong, the witness will be recalled. I think Mr. Telling is with us now. Let him be sworn, and we will hear what he has to say."

Elya's acute, erratic perception became aware that she had roused the Council's advocate to a smouldering fury which nearly caused him to pick up his papers and leave the court. He had not doubted that he would be allowed to conduct the case in his own way to his own end. He did not regard the Bench as hostile to himself, or certainly so to the application which he had made, but he thought his own dignity to be disregarded, if not contemned. He was right in this, except that contempt might have been too strong a word to express Elya's attitude to himself. He was an amusement to her.

So she had a good hope that Mr. Telling would prove to be. He was a small man, self-important, bald-headed, rotund. He was not one to disclaim responsibility, nor to be diffident concerning a decision which he had made. As he had not been called as a witness by either side, no one rose to question him, and he found himself being examined at once by Lady Lucie, before whom he had been previously, when she had given the Council her support against lesser men.

Now she said, with a smiling amiability in which no dissimulation lay—but how should he guess that it was due to her fascinated appreciation of the oddities of mankind?—"Mr. Telling, we…I have been asked to make an order for the demolition of a house which Mr. John Corbett has built for his own use. It is a matter concerning which you have special knowledge and responsibility. I also understand that it is primarily through you that the matter has been brought before us. In the event of this order being made, shall you be able to offer the defendant equal or better accommodation?"

The witness grinned an appreciation of what Mr. Corbett's position would be likely to be. "He can go on the list," he said. "He'll be treated fair."

"A list of people who are waiting for houses? And how many would be in front of him?"

"About two hundred, it might be. Or ten times that. It's a question of how many kids he's got."

"Then there are not nearly enough houses for those who need them?"

"We're doing the best we can."

"But you are asking me to destroy one already built?"

"He'd no right to build it without asking us. He must have known that."

"You appreciate that it was his own land, at his own cost, and for his own use?"

"It was against the law, for all that."

"But is it a law which you are bound to enforce? Would you have incurred any penalty if you had left him alone?"

"I couldn't say about that."

"Perhaps Mr. Atkinson will be able to help us there."

Mr. Atkinson rose to do so. He was annoyed at the direction which the questions were taking, which seemed pointless or worse than that, and it was a feeling which he saw no occasion to hide. "There is naturally no question of penalty against the Building Committee. Penalties are for those who do not observe the law."

Elya turned to the witness. "Then you were under no obligation to bring this application at all?"

Mr. Atkinson rose unasked. "I submit that the Council is under an implied obligation to assert its authority. I submit also, with due respect..."—was there sarcasm in the tone in which this was said?—"...that it may be better for me to deal with such points as these, by which the witness is being taken somewhat out of his depth."

"The witness," Elya replied, "has admitted primary responsibility for an application which sounds insane, and it is surely in his own interest to ascertain what reasons he may have had. You should not overlook that, as the case appears now, it might lead to his being consigned to a mental home."

"I must protest most strenuously," the barrister replied, in a voice of indignant astonishment, "against such an interpretation of the witness's evidence. He has brought a matter before the court in which it is submitted that the law has been broken, and the authority of the District Council has been treated with contempt, and he should be able to rely upon your support."

"But what he is asking me to do is to pull down a house. Do you seriously argue that people would rather be homeless than that the Council should be ignored?"

"They should certainly learn that they can only ignore it at their own risk."

"Mr. Atkinson, you are a barrister. You do know that that was not what I asked. And we both know…"—as she said this she looked with a confidential smile at the maddened man—"…why you didn't reply. I don't wish to be rude to you. You may have as much sense as anyone else. Leonard told me—he's a barrister like yourself—that you all argue things that you don't believe. I suppose you sometimes think it's your duty—or is it because they pay you?—to represent someone who isn't right in the head. But it isn't any use, and doesn't show much respect to the court, to talk as though you think I'm as mad as he. You must know that, apart from it being such a crazy idea to pull down houses that people need, that you're asking me to do a dishonest thing. Don't you see that it's robbery with violence if I give you permission to pull down Mr. Corbett's house, without ordering you to compensate him for the property which you would destroy?"

But Mr. Atkinson did not respond to the friendly, almost bantering tone in which this question was put. He glared for a moment of angry silence, wondering whether the flippant suggestion of insanity which had been made might not be seriously applied to the magistrate from whom it had so groundlessly proceeded. There was something *wrong* about Lady Lucie. He was conscious, without analysing, that the rhythm of her speech would change at times, as when she had said "Leonard told me"—whoever Leonard might be!—for though the thorough manner in which a conscientious angel had learned the language might result in her being able to speak with exactness as English magistrates are accustomed to do, yet, when her mind returned to herself, or her own affairs, rhythm and vocabulary would become those which her own buoyant personality found most natural for self-expression.

"I regret," he said, with the aloof dignity which he felt that the occasion required, "that you leave me no alternative but to withdraw from the case." And, as he spoke, he gathered up his papers, and left the court.

Elya looked after him with a laughter which she saw no occasion to check. She turned her eyes back to the witness to say: "Well, Mr. Telling, I don't suppose you're too loony—that word isn't really good English, it's something about the moon, but I expect you'll know what I mean; anyway, Laura used it to me—I don't suppose you're too loony to see that I've done your Council a good turn. When he gets over his sulks, I shouldn't think he'd have the cheek to ask for a fee from them, and if he should, I should suppose they'd have the sense not to pay, but nobody'd bet much on that, after the way they're behaving now. But I'm not going to waste any more time questioning you. It's time to close down and have some tea. The case is dismissed as frivolous and vexatious—I don't wish to use a stronger word—with costs for Mr. Corbett, which his neighbours will have to pay, which is hard on them, but not unjust, because they should have elected people with more sense, though I can see that they might not have been easy to find. You can tell them from me that they can appeal if they want to make you look like a public fool for a second time. I should say the dark one will win by a short head, though he started last."

The final words alluded to three reporters, who had leapt up from their seats as this judgement was delivered, with frantic consciousness that there were only two telephone booths in the outer hall.

CHAPTER TWENTY-TWO

A QUIET EVENING

Elya looked round a court which was rapidly clearing. She was aware of a murmur of many excited voices in the corridor, and was not displeased. She had the contentment of those who have done well, and have found pleasure in what they did. But a busy time was before her still, and (unless she should hurry her next meal, which she would be most unwilling to do) there was not a moment to lose.

She called the usher, paid him for the buns, asked him in how few minutes ("no, I didn't ask in how many minutes, I asked how *few*") he could have a good meal ready for her, and told him to speak at once to the dark slim gentleman who was sitting at the end of the third row on the left, and didn't seem in any hurry to go, and say that Lady Lucie would like a word with him before he left.

On this invitation, Rodney came up to the dais, waited a moment while Elya said good-bye to Mr. Thompson, who showed the soundness of his heart by remarking that the day had been an exceptional pleasure to him, and then found himself (with even more bewilderment than he had experienced as he had watched Lady Lucie preside in a manner which would have been natural to Elya, but was foreign to anything he had known of her, and with occasional allusions which only Elya would be likely to make), looking at one who was Lady Lucie in every detail, and yet spoke to him as one whom she could not be.

"Rodney," she said, "I just wanted to tell you that I—I mean Miss Gabriel—will not be back at the Red Bull till rather late. She's got a good deal to do. But there won't be any need to hurry away, because everything's gone just as she meant it should. If you're tired, you can go to bed, and wait for her there. She wants to have one more good night together before she goes back to London, and may meet other men. I can't stop talking longer. Of course, I didn't mean that. I mean can't stop longer talking, because tea must be ready now, but I hope you've enjoyed watching justice done in an English court, probably for the first time that it ever was."

"I hope it's not been quite as bad as that."

"It may not be as bad as it sounds. They do the best they can, more or less, if it's agreed that they've all got to dance in a set way. But we've no time to talk about that. I must get some tea."

He heard this last remark, and a doubt was flown, though wonder might still remain. It was the authentic Elya with whom he spoke.

But she was in a disguise which it was clear that it would be inopportune for her to leave, and he went back to the hotel with no further words, to await what the end might be. And Elya, after the unhurried meal on which she had been so firmly resolved, took Lady Lucie's car, as it was natural for her to do, and drove to that Lady's residence. A kind-hearted young angel, however sportive, cannot be entirely easy in mind when she has left a lady she is impersonating trussed up in her own bedroom for about ten hours, even though a notice not to disturb has been hung on the door. She might have escaped or have been released, and there would be complications in that. She might—but it is wrong to harbour depressing thoughts—she might even be dead!

It was at least clear, as Elya entered the house, that the lady had not escaped. All was peaceful and quiet, and whatever intention she may have had of hurrying to release her victim disappeared into forgetfulness when she became aware that a parlour-maid, following routine, had a meal laid for her return. The incident of the late substantial tea disappeared from her mind, and she sat down to the lamb chops which were hurried in, with the eagerness that the hungry feel.

She would doubtless have gone upstairs to release her victim as soon as the meal was done, but that, as she was peeling its final pear with the adroitness which Leonard had admired on a previous occasion, Lady Lucie, whose day-long wriggling had achieved belated success, walked into the room.

It was an awkward moment for both, and not least so far Bertha, who was entering behind her, to clear the table.

The minds of angels are more agile than those of men, and the position was less inexplicable to Elya than to those upon whom she gazed. Its complication was that she was determined not to move till she had finished the pear, and this led her to descend to human levels of mendacity, such as she would have said confidently could never become hers, even a moment before.

"Bertha," she said, "this is my sister, Miss Feedwell. You had better lay a place for her, when you have shown her the way to the spare room."

Bertha may be excused if she looked more surprise than a well-trained parlour-maid should be quick to do. She had thought herself to be well acquainted with Lady Lucie's near relatives, and the name Feedwell (which would naturally occur to the swift invention of one replete with a good meal) was unknown to her. Apart from that, anyone would have been surprised by a resemblance between the ladies which, in face at least, surpassed anything which could have been expected had they been congenital twins.

"Bertha," Lady Lucie said, with the natural courage of those who are conscious of their own rectitude, and the evil-doing of others, "I have been subjected by this person—this mountebank—to the grossest outrage. I have been tied up in my room since morning. You had better telephone for the police."

Bertha heard, but was not convinced. She looked in bewilderment at the two women, and it was unfortunate for the authentic Lucie that she was not in her own most appropriate garments, having had to clothe herself from those which remained after Elya had been supplied. It was unfortunate also that she was still dishevelled, particularly as to the head, by the indignity she had endured. It would have been wiser to do her hair with the usual elaboration, instead of allowing it to straggle as even Bertha had never seen it before. But was it a position in which prudence would be likely to hold the reins?

Bertha made no motion to obey. Her eyes went to Elya, seeking instructions from her. But then—*magna est veritas*—she remembered the door on which there had been so queer a notice, *do not disturb*, while her mistress had been out of the house—or, at least, so she would have been prepared to swear a moment before. The little seed of doubt which had been sown by the name Feedwell began to sprout, and then, as she looked at Elya, it grew with an instant vigour. Elya, as we know, had taken Lady Lucie's face, but the lady's figure had been more than she could endure—and it was a difference which was not overlooked by Bertha's wide-open eyes. But whether she would have obeyed the order she had received may not have been clear, even to her own mind, for next moment it had Elya's support.

"Yes," she said, "you can't do better than that. Ask them to send an inspector round to deal with a rather difficult family situation. But that's no reason why Miss Feedwell should stand. Let her have a chair, and get her something to eat. It may quieten her nerves if I tell her some of the things that have been happening in court today."

Fortified by these dual instructions, Bertha had no hesitation in ringing up the police station at Chelford-Boscott, where Lady Lucie's name was not lightly esteemed.

A moment later Bertha reported: "Chief-Inspector Barber says that he'll be here himself in ten minutes. I heard him shout to someone to get his car."

Elya said: "That will be just right." She saw that there would be time enough for another pear.

It is ignominious to take a seat at the side of your own table, while you are accused of impersonating yourself, and are so hungry that you can't restrain yourself from wolfing the chops which are laid before you, while the charlatan who has taken your place tells with bubbling merriment of the monstrous things that you have been made to say and do with reporters' pencils busy two yards away. But it was not for long. In less than ten minutes, Chief Inspector Barber came into the room.

He was a neat man: neat in manner, and in attire. He had a neat, orderly mind. Unimaginative, he observed the obvious, and expected it to occur. As it usually did, his reputation flourished. The inspector of fiction gains repute by postulating the improbable, by unearthing bizarre clues. But Chief Inspector Barber had a different outlook, and had come to where he was by a safer road.

Now he saw one who had the aspect of Lady Lucie seated where he was accustomed to see her sit, and the fact that there was another of very similar appearance, but not quite so well washed or groomed, seated halfway down the side of the table (a position which Bertha had wisely chosen, as it was evident that the ladies, whoever each might be, were not on such terms of amity that they could not endure to be somewhat distant from one another), and he had no doubt of who was in proper authority there.

He said, with punctilious politeness: "Good evening, my lady. I understand you've been having a little trouble?"

"Yes, we did," Elya replied, "but it's over. Miss Feedwell rather lost her head, but she's better now."

Lady Lucie broke out angrily: "Inspector, that woman isn't I. She's a clever fake. It was I who was the first to ask Bertha to ring up for you to come. I charge her with impersonation and fraud, and tying me up in my own bedroom, while she went to court in my clothes, which she's got on now."

Elya said, with real kindliness in her voice, for she was truly sorry for anyone as hungry as Lady Lucie appeared to be: "She'll be better when she's had a good meal."

"I shall be better when I've seen you sent to the cells." (The police officer was mislead by truth and....

[missing pages 210-212 of the manuscript]

...into welcome rest. "But oh! I have had a lovely time!"

CHAPTER TWENTY-THREE

RETURN TO LONDON

The human Elya had a perfect body—or should we say a succession of bodies?—which did not go short of food. It might be asked (and would not have been easily answered, even by her), why, if she changed from mortal to flea, and then into a cat, and then into girl again, should the last incarnation be weakened by the exertions of those which had gone before? But explanation (or its absence) does not alter fact, and an incarnate weariness could not be put aside by metamorphosis of whatever kind.

Now the body which had been hers only since she had got into bed was exhausted, and overslept.

Rodney remembered how late (or early) was the hour when a cat had entered the room. He let a sleeping loveliness lie undisturbed till a late hour, and then found ready assent to a proposal that she should have breakfast in bed.

But he found her to be resolute in determination that they should return to London without further delay. She said that she had a duty to the Chinese Embassy which she could not ignore. "And besides," she said, "I must have some fun, or I shall just throw it all up, and you'd never see me again. How should you like that?"

He owned that he wouldn't like that at all, though his judgement told him that he had been drawn—and how willingly!—into an adventure which could not last. And meanwhile Elya issued her next order, in a manner which was too casual to be rude. "I'm not going back by rail. It's too dull. You must get a car."

"I could hire one, if you mean that."

"I mean whatever you'll have to do. But you'd better telephone for it at once, while we have something to eat. Yes I know. But I've dressed since then. Do you expect me never to eat?"

So he hired the car obediently, and Elya was soon seated at his left hand, watching him drive. She saw the deadly necessity of allowing him to concentrate on what he did. "Of course," she thought, "I am safe. But for him, and those with whom he may at any moment collide, is it that they don't care, or that they are too stupid to understand anything that they haven't seen—till it's too late to matter?"

But next moment her mind had turned to something of more consequence to herself, and of an urgency she would not defer.

She asked: "You saw that woman with yellow hair dyed darker on one side than the other, and the nose that no one could ever deserve to have?"

"I saw a rather pretty blonde. What about her?"

"There was a man with her. He had a dirty patch on his left sleeve."

"I didn't notice that. But I know the man whom you mean."

"Did he pay her?"

"It is a possibility."

"How much?"

"How could I say?"

"Well, I want to know."

"He probably paid the hotel bill. He may have given her a present as well."

"I mean money."

"You can't expect me to know that."

"Would it be as much as ten pounds?"

"It might be more."

"We'll say ten. I shall want a lot more than she. Shall we say ten times as much, or is that being too rude to me?"

"Do you want me to give you a hundred pounds?"

"It's not what I want. It's what you ought to do. She couldn't have been nearly as good as I. I've got good technique. I don't say: 'Have you put out the cat?' just at the wrong moment, as I know some women do."

"No. I'll give you that. Though I mightn't know whether you were talking about yourself if you did."

"Yes. I see that. It wasn't quite the best illustration to use. But you know what I mean. Suppose we say eighty, unless you'd feel too bad about it not being more?"

"You needn't fear that."

"Then I won't. We'll say eighty, and you can let me have a cheque as soon as we get by ourselves. Not before. You can come up to my flat. When we've had a meal, I shall want you to take me there."

"I can do that."

"And will it be too late to open a bank account afterwards?"

"I'm afraid it will."

"Then that must be tomorrow. I want you to show me how to do it. But I think I know. Your friends give you references, and then you do the same for them. And the bankers believe it all. I'm glad I've got plenty of friends. I shall say Sir Eden and you. Sir Andrew may be feeling tired of me. It isn't easy to guess. And Leonard wouldn't say quite enough. I couldn't risk Laura either. Now she thinks Leonard's done with me (but it was the other way round), she'd love to call me the worst names she knows. Her trouble'd be that there are so many she doesn't!"

"I haven't met Laura, so it isn't easy to guess. Some women know more than you'd ever think. But I thought Sir Andrew to be about the best friend you've got."

"You may be right. But I think he's a man who has moods. Of course, I should manage him if it were worthwhile. But Sir Eden ought to be good enough. Does he always smoke those cigars? I heard someone say that they're bad for something inside. I ought to have learned more about that. But what a nuisance insides must be. You'd be almost like angels except for them. I might have done him a good turn. Why do people mix yellows and pinks in their garden flowers? I expect that's what you ought to mean by the Fall of Man. It might have been a Rise but for that."

The last remark was induced by the sight of gardens bright with early June flowers at the side of the road. It sounded absurd to Rodney, as Elya's articulated ruminations frequently would, but on reflection he saw more meaning than could be quickly observed. The evolution of man, call it fall or rise, had caused him to attempt control of his environment, through which he produced ugliness or disharmony of colour, such as Nature, in its apparent blindness, would never do. Was there no meaning in that?

It occurred to him that he had been singularly lacking in intellectual enterprise. If she were angel indeed, which there was some reason to think, why had he asked her nothing concerning celestial things, on which she must have knowledge denied to men?

It was an omission to be corrected at once. He asked, and found her as ready to talk on that as on any other subject which might intrude.

"How the Earth was made? I know how silly men are, but you won't make me believe that they're so loony they can't see that. If you know how you make things, you must know how they are made. You think first, and you get ideas, and then you build or carve or dig, to make what you thought. Or you may want an animal to have longer legs, and you plan for that.

"And when you've built, you think of something you'd like to add, and you begin planning again.

"If you can't see that that's how the Earth was made into the live thing that it is now, you must be weak in the head.

"It wasn't all done at once, or thought out. There've been a lot of experiments that have had to go. Dozens were worth keeping on, even after the idea came to have creatures walking about. But mastodons weren't. They had to go, whether they liked it or not. And so would humans, I suppose, if there were a better idea. But I'm beginning to talk about things you know more about than an angel. We know what and where we are, and what more can we want?"

She ceased to talk. She looked alertly ahead. Those vehicles *must collide*. So they did. The lorry turned the car over across their path. Rodney swerved sharply, but it would have been in vain, even had they not begun to skid.

He was conscious that a heap of clothes collapsed at his side, and that was the last thing that he lived to know.

ABOUT THE AUTHOR

SYDNEY FOWLER WRIGHT (1874-1965) penned over seventy volumes of science fiction, fantasy, classic mysteries, historical novels, poetry, and non-fiction, many of them being published by the Borgo Press Imprint of Wildside Press.

www.ingramcontent.com/pod-product-compliance
Lightning Source LLC
Chambersburg PA
CBHW050730250626
47155CB00005B/1734